ISBN: 9798858171300

Katy Wimhurst 2023

© TM ®

Alien Buddha Press 2023

Let Them Float

And Other Short Stories

Katy Wimhurst

abuddhapress@yahoo.com

The following are works of fiction. Any similarities to actual

people, places, or events, unless deliberately expressed otherwise

by the author, are purely coincidental.

Contents

5

4

3

2

1

Let Them Float

It was like any walk to work through Castle Park until something tugged at Isla's attention. She halted, cupping her hand to her mouth. *Jeez.*

A woman was floating upright above a leafy oak tree. Her slender arms were opened a little on each side, like a half-baked ballet pose. She wore blue jeans and a matching jacket, and she stared skyward blankly, her chin tilted up. Suspended in the air, she resembled a figure from a Chagall painting or a lost angel in denim. What was she doing up there?

Would this be like the epidemic of Fainters in town, from a couple of years back? Or a few years before that, the Hornies, the group of teenagers who sprouted goat's horns on their heads – Isla's nephew, Hamish, aged five at the time, loved those.

From where Isla stood, the floating woman looked twenty-something. *Does she have any children*? A question Isla asked herself about many strangers. She reached for her neck scarf and absent-mindedly rubbed its silky material between her thumb and forefinger. Three men ahead of her had stopped, one filming the woman on his phone. Isla would have loved to linger and watch, but another busy day at work awaited. She tore herself away.

In the sunlight, the wrought-iron park gates threw shadows like pretty lattices onto St Peter's Street. Isla's office was in a glass-fronted building halfway down this road. In the foyer, the sign above Reception read: *Orizone: Compliments for Condiments.* She wrote copy for a marketing company specialising in foods such as chutneys and pickles; hardly a dream job. Her boyfriend, Gaitlin, jokingly called her the 'chutney champion'.

Kylie, the smiley receptionist with a ginger bob, greeted her.

'Heard about the floating woman?' asked Isla.

9

'Pardon?' Kylie's brow creased as Isla explained. 'I'm definitely going to have a nosey at lunchtime. What's that all about?'

'Wish I knew.' Isla glanced at Kylie's telephone. 'Any calls for me?'

Kylie's brows rose. 'That Mr Lancaster *again*. I told him to try in half an hour.'

A difficult client, Isla's heart plummeted.

Sunlight sluiced through the floor-to-ceiling windows in the open-plan office. As ever, Isla was the earliest to arrive. She put her velvet jacket on the back of her chair while looking at a silver-framed photo on her desk. It showed her nephew in a school uniform, smiling in his sweet, bashful way. All the other women her age here had photos of their own kids on display. Isla switched on her desktop and turned her attention to her emails. Four already from Mr Lancaster. *Oh, spare me*. She clicked on his first one and tried to concentrate, but her mind harked back to the floating woman.

That night, Isla arrived home late again. The UNICEF calendar on the hallway wall had her birthday next month, June 21st, circled in pink felt-tip. Almost a year past the milestone of forty. Would the next decade also involve being a chutney champion? That idea made her feel flat as a tack. Over the last few years, she'd applied for several other jobs, with no luck.

The jacket on the back of the armchair and Anglia News playing quietly on the television signalled that Gaitlin had already arrived. They'd been a couple for three years and spent three nights a week together.

In the narrow kitchen, next to the living room, Gaitlin was chopping vegetables. His tightly cropped blond hair haloed a pale round face with thin-rimmed circular glasses. He looked like a canny moon – though wasn't remotely lunar – and he was in a white work shirt, sleeves rolled up. He was a head taller than Isla, as well as chunkier, with what he termed a 'middle-aged middle'.

'Have you seen this?' Isla indicated the television, on which the news featured the floating woman.

10

'Good to see you, too.'

'Hey, you,' she said with a brief smile. 'This woman above Castle Park, though.' She pointed again.

He stopped chopping and frowned over at the screen. 'Oh, that.'

'You don't wonder about her?' The woman had been there all day.

'You won't get worked up about her, will you? Like you did about those Fainters.'

Isla knew Gaitlin was asking for his sake, not hers. He wasn't an emotionally supportive boyfriend, but did at least express his love via his cooking. 'What's for dinner, then?' she said, changing the subject.

'Chicken korma, black rice, and fennel salad.'

'Sounds good.'

The news had moved on to another story, so Isla turned the volume right down. When she opened the French windows onto the tiny balcony off the living room, the cool evening air offered a tonic. The metal railings penned in numerous potted plants. 'How are you, my babies?' she said.

'Not talking to them again, are you?' called Gaitlin.

'They like it,' she called back.

On the second floor of the grey-brick flats opposite, someone had a sign in the window: *Never Vote Tory*. Isla found it amusing, but Gaitlin didn't.

Her gaze came to rest on the silver birch tree in the distance, which shimmered like liquid metal, and the floating woman pushed into her mind again. *God, I'm obsessed with her. Is that normal?* She wondered if other women, those with children, fretted about such things or if they were too busy to care.

***

'Mummy. Look.' Gareth stopped and pointed.

Nadine glanced up. *What the actual fuck?* A woman hovered above a tree, like a human cloud. Her arms were stretched out, half-assed, and she looked pretty

11

out of it. Stoned maybe – not that Nadine could recall what that was like. Would the woman fall? Nadine imagined her tumbling from the sky and landing with a *thwack*, akin to that cartoon coyote. *Ouch.*

'Awesome. She's flying, Mummy,' said Christos.

'How come she can float?' asked Gareth.

'No idea.' Nadine remembered the Hornies from a few years back. Would this be a freak show similar to that?

Her boys, who spent half their lives squabbling, became all quiet and open-mouthed. Nadine took a shot of the woman on her phone and then saw the time: 5 pm. *Damn.* They were already late and their car was on the far side of Castle Park. 'Come on. We need to go.'

'No. I want to watch.' Gareth often played up before she took them to Javier's for the weekend; this was more understandable.

'Come *on.*' Nadine wanted to stay too but had to get to work.

Fifteen minutes later, they arrived by car at Hoban House, a modern block where Javier lived alone in a ground-floor flat. Armed with the boys' bags, she hurried them to the main door, rang the buzzer, and kissed them both. 'Love you.'

Javier, in a blue polo shirt, a slight nick on his chin telling her he'd just shaved, wore his familiar aftershave; odd for him to put that on for the boys. She'd got pregnant by accident after they'd fallen in love during her first year of a degree in Spanish; he was in his final year of doing business studies. His Catholicism and Nadine being besotted with him meant she had to drop out of university. By the time Javier completed his master's degree, they had both their boys.

'Daddy.' Christos hugged his father.

'Hi, boys.' Javier ruffled their hair.

Nadine handed over the bags.

'There's a woman in the park, Daddy,' said Gareth. 'She's flying.'

As Nadine explained, Javier's head tilted to one side. 'How intriguing,' he said.

That was odd for Javier, master of the existential shrug. 'Why not take the boys to see the woman over the weekend if she's still there?' she said.

'Hmm. Not sure.'

Now *that* was more like him. When they first dated, Nadine was wowed by his 'coolness', only later realising he was more self-absorbed than Zen. How had she ever been so infatuated? Javier was certainly hot and smart, but banging on endlessly about 'resource management', and not really listening when she gushed about Lorca or other writers discovered on her degree, hardly made him ideal, even as student boyfriend material. He'd taken her home to Barcelona, though, and showed her the Miro Museum and Park Guelle. She was bowled over and even got the name of his favourite indie band, La Buena Vida, tattooed on her arm – what an idiot!

'Remember swimming tomorrow at 4 pm,' Nadine said. She booked the kids' lessons at a time when Javier would have to take them; he wasn't good at doing things with them.

'*Si. Yo se.*' Javier reverted to Spanish when pissed off.

And *that* always irritated her.

Nadine dashed home in the car. She scooped up the Lego from the kitchen table, tidying it away. Just time for a cuppa and a sarnie before her shift tonight. She also wolfed down a chocolate pudding, a Mars Bar, and four Quality Street. Then came the obligatory dose of self-loathing: *why can't I stop shovelling chocolate down myself?*

The Queen's Head on Greenmore Estate filled up quickly on a Friday evening. The pub, dating back to Edwardian times, had an older clientele. It stank of beer, played 80s pop music, and the wooden tables were scratched with decades-old marks, like an indecipherable script. Nadine wondered if she'd be stuck working in this dump forever. The vision of a school in the mediaeval part of Barcelona, with its lanes and gothic architecture, appeared in her mind; the students looked on eagerly as she taught them how to conjugate a verb: *I am, you are…*

'What does it take to get a beer round here?' barked a voice. At the bar, a man was waving a tenner. 'You seemed off with the fairies, love. Two pints of lager, please.'

As she served the drinks, Nadine overheard the conversation between the man and his friend.

'Seen this crackpot above the park?' The customer held up his phone.

'Levitating zombie more like, mate.' The friend chortled.

'What's she up to, then?' the man said.

'Could be a religious crank.'

It was a hectic evening. Nadine arrived home at midnight. Though knackered, she was hyper and couldn't sleep. On her phone, she pored over the photos of the floating woman posted to the town's Facebook page, and read the comments in the threads:

It's Janey Townsend. She was in my class at school. A weirdo. Not surprised she's still a freak.

Harry Kennet dated her in the sixth form and said she was a terrible kisser.

Don't be so judgmental, you lot!!! Remember what a brainbox she was?

Nadine posted a comment too: *The last poster has a point. Stop being mean to the poor woman!* Then she added: *And given this town (Fainters, Hornies, etc.), do people think there might soon be others joining her up there?*

***

As soon as he heard the front door click, Malcolm looked up from *The Daily Express*. Sooty leapt up and dashed to the lounge door, her tail going ten to the dozen, as Sheila, in that navy fleece of hers, entered the room.

'Hello,' she said, as she bent down to pet Sooty.

'Those immigrants are coming over in dinghies again.' Malcolm waved his paper. 'A hundred arrived yesterday. A hundred.' It was hard enough already to book an appointment with Dr Lambton. Last time, it'd taken two whole weeks to get in to see the GP. This boatload would make it worse.

'Had my hair done. A new style. How does it look?'

Typical Sheila. Always ignored him when he talked about important stuff. He glanced at the short grey curls framing her round face with its double chin. 'Doesn't look that different to me.'

'Hmm.' She adjusted her heavy-rimmed glasses. 'I need to sort out the shopping. You couldn't take the frozen food out to the garage, could you?'

He looked at the mantelpiece clock. 'I should walk Sooty.'

'Right,' she said flatly and vanished.

Sooty came over to Malcolm. 'Who's my good girl?' he said, stroking her. He stood. 'Come on, you.' Sooty's wagging tail bumped against his leg.

'Off now!' he called, before shutting the front door.

Clouds like dirty dishcloths hung in the sky, and it was nippy for mid-May, making his arthritic left knee ache. Nice to be out, though. Afternoon walks gave him something to do since he'd retired from his job as a taxi driver. He missed the banter of the other drivers, if not the waiting at taxi ranks.

Mercers Drive was lined with semi-detached 1960s houses like Malcolm and Sheila's and ended at Castle Park. That place was sprinkled with lime trees and oaks, with a big old Norman castle at the top. Alice, his granddaughter, couldn't get enough of it. In Lower Castle Park, a crowd – about two dozen people – gathered by the little boating pond. 'What's all that about?' he said to Sooty.

Moving closer, he spotted a camera crew and a reporter, their noses all poking into the air. Looking up, too, Malcolm stopped dead. A woman was there, right above an oak. He shook his head in disdain, fisted his hands on his hips. *Women shouldn't float like that. They just shouldn't.*

'Cool, isn't it? She's been there all day.' A lad who had one of those stupid floppy fringes was standing nearby.

'Hmph.'

The lad pointed. 'Anglia News is doing a feature on her.'

15

The woman – who looked like a youngster – stared off into the distance, her face blank. At that age, Malcolm had a family to support and fourteen-hour taxi shifts. No way would he have been loafing around above a tree. 'Probably one of those benefits scroungers,' he told Sooty.

Not wanting to hang about with the groupies, he quit the park in a hurry and did the river walk instead.

Back home, the kitchen smelled of Bolognese cooking. Anglia News was on the small television, and Sheila was glued to the set. A shot showed the woman hovering above the tree.

'I saw her when I walked Sooty.'

'Shush,' she said. 'I'm trying to listen.'

He took a beer from the fridge, removed the bottle top, and poured it fizzing into a glass. 'Hasn't she got somewhere to be, a job?'

'I said, I'm trying to listen.'

Malcolm's thoughts flicked to those Fainters of two years back. A bunch of hysterical women – well, mainly women – who kept fainting on buses, in shops, in cafes. He'd clocked the rubbish himself in Tesco, five women at different points along the biscuit aisle, each with a supermarket trolley, all dropping to the ground, one after another. 'Get up. Stop being ridiculous,' he'd wanted to say, tense with annoyance. Too much pandering to such types these days. Back in his day, you just got on with things; you had no choice. The fainting had spread like chicken pox, but the council was way too flaky in response.

'They need to nip this floating in the bud,' he told Sheila.

She used the remote to turn the volume up, and Malcolm retreated to the haven of the living room.

At 6.30 pm, Sheila came in to tell him dinner was ready. As they tucked in, she said, 'Do you like the Bolognese?'

'It's okay. Bit too much salt, maybe.' Sheila wasn't the best cook, though admittedly better than he was.

Sheila's brow creased. 'On the television, it said she's an athlete. A long-distance runner.'

'Who?'

'That floating woman.'

'Oh.' Malcolm ate another mouthful. Quite good, actually.

'And clever. Studied philosophy at university, apparently.'

'The council should get her down.'

Sheila stood abruptly and took her plate to the sink.

'What's for pud?' he asked.

She opened the fridge. 'Fruit salad.'

'Not got any of that nice Tesco's sticky toffee pudding?'

'I made a fruit salad.' She took out the bowl and shut the fridge door hard.

'Careful.'

As they ate pudding, he asked, 'Are we going round to Kylie's on Saturday?'

She nodded. 'I'll bake an apple pie.'

'Good.' Malcolm enjoyed going to his daughter's house but mainly to see his granddaughter. He spent hours playing board games with Alice, usually letting her thrash him – he loved that girl to bits.

'I take it you're watching the football later?' said Sheila.

'Course.' Malcolm never missed an Arsenal game on the television.

'I'll pop out with Sooty, then.'

'Why?'

'I want to see that woman.'

'If you ask me, they should drag her down somehow.'

'They aren't asking you, though, are they?' She stared, her mouth pinched into a tight line.

'Everything alright, Sheila?'

She stood and hovered for a moment, as if about to say something, and then hurried to the sink. 'Sorry, I'm not feeling myself.' She sorted out the dishes.

17

During the match's half-time, he heard Sheila and Sooty return through the front door. Annoyed that Arsenal was losing 2-0, he padded through to the kitchen to get a mint.

'She's still there. It's a nice evening but chilly out.' Sheila was in her navy fleece.

'Arsenal's having a 'mare.'

'Oh, dear.'

'Don't worry about that woman. She'll come to her senses in a day or so.'

'But she looks lonely. Perhaps someone should join her.'

'Maybe *you* should.' Malcolm chuckled at the joke and returned to the television.

***

Apart from the odd *vox pop* speculating on how the floating woman might survive up there, how she might drink or pee, the local media quickly stopped paying her heed. Isla, who checked the news and Facebook feeds daily, wondered if this was a lack of concern or denial. Interest peaked again a few days later, though, when another woman appeared above an adjacent oak tree.

The park was under an overcast, gloomy sky on the day Isla witnessed this. The second woman was plump and had cartoonishly thick glasses, a brown skirt that billowed in the breeze, and grey hair that suggested she was way too old to be a mother. Just like the first one, she floated in an upright position, her arms slightly open and her chin tilted towards the heavens. The spectacle had a touch of comedy, akin to Monty Python reimagining Chagall's art. The second woman wore a navy fleece which would keep her warmer. Isla worried about the one in denim being freezing cold at night.

Isla spent fifteen minutes on a park bench, mesmerised by the two Floaters. Neither acknowledged the other nor the spectators below. Were they in a trance or just indifferent?

When Gaitlin came to her flat later, she asked, 'Did you see the second woman today?'

'One woman is plenty enough for me,' he joked, hanging his jacket on a hallway peg. His boyish smile shaved a decade off his forty-one years.

'I mean the floating one in the park.'

He followed her through to the living room. 'Is there another?'

'Aye, Sherlock.'

He stopped at her bookcase for a minute, frowning, and then lifted a book from it. 'Why do you read this leftie stuff?' He held up *Capitalism And Bullshit Jobs*.

Whenever she carped at him a little, he had to niggle back somehow. 'Don't start,' she said. He was super confident in his opinions, while she, even when the world had seemed more anchored than she found it these days, had room for doubt. Isla still loved Gaitlin's large grey eyes, which desperately tried to pin order on a world that may not have much. She loved his food fanaticism and the manner in which he teased her, but he rubbed her up the wrong way, too. She'd considered ending things but had been single for several years before meeting him – except for some unpleasant flings with cads from an internet dating site. Gaitlin, who she was introduced to at a friend's party, was far preferable to them.

'This was between Kafka and Hans Christian Andersen.' Gaitlin held up the book. 'Politics next to fairy tales. Can't you keep anything in order?' A teasing tone.

'Kafka isn't a fairy tale.'

'It's still Grimm.' He smiled at his own pun and put the book back. He then reached into his jacket pocket and brought out a tiny box. 'I got you something.'

Inside was a 5cm seahorse carved from wood and painted pale orange. 'Och, he's a wee cutie,' said Isla. 'To what do I owe this?'

'Just saw it in the window of Traders East and thought you'd like Pygmy 20.'

'Pygmy 21, actually.' She'd collected wee seahorse ornaments since childhood, loving how delicate and improbable the animals were, and named them all Pygmy. She placed this one on the shelf with all the others, then kissed Gaitlin on the cheek. 'Thanks,' she said. Sometimes he surprised her. 'Like some wine?'

'Please.'

In the kitchen, Isla took the bottle out of the fridge and poured two glasses. 'Here.' She handed one to Gaitlin. 'Why do you think there's a second woman floating?' she asked, expecting him to change the subject.

He sipped his wine. 'Mollie's with me next Tuesday as Andrea is away in Dublin, so I'll stay at my place, okay?'

'Okay.' The second bedroom in Isla's flat was a box room. That Gaitlin had a teenage daughter from his last relationship, who spent a few nights a week with him, offered Isla a convenient excuse for never inviting him to move in here.

'Mollie scored 52 runs today.' His eyes lit up with pride. His daughter was the star of a girls' cricket team.

'That's great.'

'She's got a tournament next Saturday. I've promised to drive her up, so I'll be gone most of the day. That's alright, isn't it?'

The only thing he was sensitive about was that Isla didn't have kids to occupy her, too. The hysterectomy following cancer in her early thirties had seen to that. 'It's fine. I'll see if I can take Hamish out.' Isla took a sip of wine. 'My sister texted earlier to ask if you'd make Hamish's birthday cake again. A banana one. He'll be ten on the 25th,' she said.

'Yup, love to.'

'Thanks. What are we having for dinner tonight?'

Gaitlin put his glass down and squeezed past her to get to the fridge. He opened it and rubbed his hands together. 'There's salmon left. I thought I'd pan fry it with dill and sesame and make a carrot salad to go with.'

'Sounds good.'

That he made such an effort with the cooking pleased her. Their relationship was more of an alliance than a perfect match. The coexistence of two lonelinesses. They were like two jigsaw puzzles – one of a football pitch, one of a garden – kept in the same box, and sometimes the pieces fitted together somehow. She knew she was playing safe, but at her age, her approach was pragmatic, too. Most relationships involved compromise. Isla had only adored one man passionately, Manos, and look at how that ended. Recalling Manos stirred up sadness, making Isla glug her wine.

***

When Nadine picked up the kids on Sunday from Javier's, a fancy yellow sports car was in his parking space. Who did that thing belong to? Javier wasn't into cars.

Gareth was quieter than usual, Christos more hyper. Driving up Lexden Road, she asked, 'Did Daddy take you to see the women in Castle Park?'

'No, but I know there's another,' said Gareth. 'Can we go tomorrow? Please, Mummy.'

'Please,' Christos echoed.

'After school. I want to see them, too.' Nadine had checked out early photos of the second one on Facebook, who looked like a stoned granny. Thoughts about the Floaters sometimes snuck into Nadine's brain. Better than being obsessed with chocolate.

'We went to Jimmy's Farm,' Christos said.

'Really?' That didn't sound like Javier, as it was a thirty-minute drive. It used to take hard-core nagging to get him to go on any trips, even to see his folks. Javier's reluctance to do things together as a family was a crucial reason their marriage bit the dust. Back then, Nadine often tried to talk to him about it, but he'd get shirty, claiming she made a mountain out of a molehill. 'You're the mountain – of stubbornness,' she'd say. But he suffered from social anxiety, too.

'Which animal did you like best?' she asked the boys.

21

'The goats,' said Gareth.

'The bunny rabbits were cute.' Christos giggled. 'Hope liked the bunnies best, too.'

'Hope?'

'Daddy's got a new girlfriend,' muttered Gareth.

Anger sizzled through Nadine. Why the hell hadn't he told her in advance that a new girlfriend would meet the kids? How like him! Nadine tried to keep the irritation from her voice: 'So, what's she like?'

'Her car is sporty, and she owns a cat called Dumbledore after Harry Potter,' said Christos.

'She likes books?' asked Nadine.

'She'll be twenty-three soon and has a horse called Minus,' said Christos.

'Midas, like the golden king,' Gareth corrected.

Six years younger than Nadine, eight than Javier. No kids, probably, and a horse. *Lucky cow.* Given the free time Javier had on weekday evenings, Nadine had long known he was more likely than her to meet someone new. When did she have the chance to date? Even two years on from them breaking up, this still felt like a kick in the proverbial.

'I don't like the name Hope,' said Gareth.

It's better than 'Fed Up'. That could be her middle name: Nadine Fed Up Cabrera. She had kept Javier's surname, which in Spanish meant 'the place of the goats'. Nadine Fed Up Cabrera imagined an arid valley filled with unhappy goats and her.

Christos's words broke the bubble of her thoughts. 'There's a birthday party for Hope at Daddy's soon,' he said. 'Hope's going to invite you too, Mummy.'

Oh, please, no. Part of Nadine was intrigued to discover what the woman was like, though.

Gareth still seemed subdued, Christos too eager. Of the two, Gareth had been more upset by his parents' split and would occasionally ask, 'Will you and Daddy ever get back together?'

'No,' she'd say. 'But we'll both *always* be here for you and your brother.'

Home was a rented, terraced, redbrick cottage in a quiet lane. Nadine texted Javier when she got there to say he should have told her and the boys in advance about the new girlfriend. She'd done two loads of washing before he texted back to say that they knew now and both boys loved meeting Hope. She was tempted to reply *NOT TRUE* but stopped herself.

Nadine prepared the boys' tea, catching the end of Anglia News. How gutting to have missed the story about the Floaters; she wanted to know the name of the second one.

As she opened the fridge door, a drawing pinned there fell off. She picked it up – a piece by Christos, titled, 'My Mummy'. Her boy was good at art – the cupid's bow on her upper lip, the espresso-brown bob and fringe, and the big green eyes captured something of her, although the slim body was, ahem, wishful thinking. She reattached the picture with a magnet.

During tea, Gareth mentioned it was his friend Hamish's birthday soon. 'He'll be ten. I need a present.'

Damn. Another expense. Even though Javier paid his child maintenance reliably, Nadine was always juggling money. She didn't enjoy taking Gareth to Hamish's, either. Hamish himself was a sweet boy, but his parents, both lawyers with airs and graces, lived in one of those la-di-da houses on Oaks Drive. 'Let's pop into town tomorrow after school. We can combine it with seeing the Floaters.'

'How come there are two up there now?' asked Gareth.

'A good question,' said Nadine.

'Isn't it against gravity?'

'Another good question.'

After tea, Nadine's gut played up – IBS often gave her gyp – and she took Rennie tablets, microwaved a heat pack and sat on the sofa near her boys, warming

23

her belly. Her mind drifted to Javier's new woman. To distract herself, she opened Facebook. *Blimey. More Floater photos.* There were more comments, too:

   I recognise the second one. She ran that florist shop on Queen Street and did the flowers for my wedding.

   What happens when they do a number 2?
   Turd drops!!
   Ffs. Don't be so disgusting.

   'What are you looking at, Mummy?' Gareth peered at her phone.
   Nadine closed the app before he could read the comments. 'Do you think we should get Hope a birthday present too when we get Hamish one?'
   'Hmm,' said Gareth.

***

The mantelpiece had a vase of pink lilies and carnations that Sheila, who used to work as a florist, put there yesterday. *Got to give it to her,* thought Malcolm. *She keeps the house looking top-notch.* Above the flowers, framed photos told the story of their life. Him in his white John Travolta suit – long ago, he had been a Tony Manero on the dance floor – and Sheila with her flicked Farrah Fawcett fringe and preggers bump showing beneath her white dress on their wedding day. Both in their early twenties there, Kylie's arrival put firm brakes on their nights out at Mimi's Discotheque. Another picture: him, Sheila, and Kylie, aged eleven, on the Spinball Whizzer ride at Alton Towers. Those were the days. And fifteen years later: Sheila and Malcolm on a beach during their first holiday to Crete. Sheila couldn't get enough of snorkelling, but he was bitten by too many mosquitoes and couldn't wait to come home from the heat. They only went abroad a few times afterwards, to that pretty mediaeval place, Bruges, which he liked.

He looked at Sooty. 'Where's she got to?' he said. Sheila had gone out that morning to visit a friend, saying she'd be back by early afternoon, and it was nearly 4 pm now. Not that he was complaining – a bit of domestic peace never went amiss, haha. He made himself a cuppa, cut a slice of fruitcake, and took a pew in the living room to read *The Daily Express*.

On the front page was another story about those migrants crossing the channel. From Sudan, it said. Malcolm once knew a taxi driver from Sudan, Hassan. Or was Hassan Libyan? Same difference. The bloke had seemed chatty and likeable at first, but then Malcolm had lost regular punters to Stansted Airport and found out Hassan was charging ten quid less. Malcolm had a right showdown with him over that. *Bloody foreigners.*

'Dad. You can't hate on a group of people just because one of them undercuts you,' Kylie scolded him, but what did she know? Malcolm knew what was what. You didn't drive a taxi for forty years without sussing out what people were like.

Sooty nuzzling at his leg reminded Malcolm that it was time to walk her. Still no Sheila. Maybe she was checking out that new garden centre on the way home. 'Let's go,' he said to Sooty.

It was a fresh afternoon, with plump clouds in the sky. The park smelled of cut grass, and a cluster of people stood near the boating pond. As Malcolm got nearer to them, Sooty began barking – unlike her. 'Behave,' he said, and she did.

Then he looked up. *Christ.* Another one was up there. His blood turned icy as he recognised the grey curly hair, tan stockings, and navy fleece. *No, no.* She'd gone to her friend's, hadn't she? He stared. It *was* her. He glanced around to see how many people were looking at her – lots! – and curbed an urge to shout up. 'Sheila,' he muttered under his breath. 'For Christ's sake. Get down.'

Sooty let out another loud woof. 'Stop it,' he snapped, and Sooty whined and wagged her tail to placate him.

What should he do? He stood, biting his lip. Thoughts whipped around his mind, like motor blades. A memory came of standing in Castle Park as a child, watching a blue balloon float into the sky. It'd been his, hadn't it? Had he let go? His mum had been there and his dad, the stupid bloke, was drunk again. Malcolm shook his head impatiently. Why waste time thinking about that nonsense now?

He took his phone out and, fingers shaking, dialled Kylie's number.

She answered. 'Dad! I'm at work.'

'It's your mum.'

'What's wrong?' Her tone changed.

'She's joined that damn Floater.' He told Kylie what was up.

'Oh, lordy. I'll be there in a jiff.'

Kylie worked at some posh marketing place on Saint Peter's Street, a stone's throw away. Within five minutes, Malcolm spotted her. Kylie had an odd way of walking – hurried and with a little skip every few steps, like she was a kid making a polite dash for the loo. As always, she looked smart, wearing a dark jacket, skirt, and high-heeled shoes.

'Dad! What on earth?' Kylie stared up at Sheila.

'Got no idea why she's up there.' He wanted to get that in before Kylie blamed him.

'Excuse me?' A brunette approached, a looker with a face full of makeup. 'I'm with Anglia News. We need local people to interview about the Floaters. Just *vox pops*. Are either of you interested?'

'No,' said Malcolm, grumpily. What had fox pups to do with his Sheila, anyway? 'That's my bl...' He swallowed the swear word. 'My wife's up there.'

Kylie's look told him that wasn't the wisest thing to say.

The brunette's eyes lit up. 'Goodness. It must be a confusing time. Might you do a brief interview? We'd love to hear what you think.'

'No.' His face and ears burned with heat. 'I've not got a clue why she's up there.'

'It would fascinate our viewers to hear your thoughts. It won't take long.'

'My dad said no,' said Kylie.

'Isn't it better to get your side of things across than have all and sundry speculating about your wife, sir?'

Malcolm didn't put up that much of a fight. In front of the camera, he kept fiddling with Sooty's leash. His mind went blank, and he only managed to say, 'I've got no idea why she's up there... like some human balloon.'

He tugged at Sooty's lead and hurried away with the dog.

***

The following weekend, four people were floating above the trees, the two already there joined by a plump woman in a pale pink tracksuit and a thin lad in a grey hoodie. Pseudo-expects appeared in the media to try to explain the phenomenon.

'It's human evolution taken to the next vibrational level,' one New Age guru claimed.

Isla rolled her eyes at that. The Floaters didn't appear to be in spiritual contemplation. She subscribed to a YouTube channel dedicated to them. Whoever ran it had a zoom lens, and close-ups of the Floaters' faces showed glazed expressions, as if all life had retreated to a distant place within them. In fact, an internet meme existed featuring a tightly-cropped facial photo of the original Floater – eyes vacant – paired with the words *not feeling it*.

Isla lay in bed at night watching the YouTube videos and running a finger absent-mindedly over the solitary feather tattoo below her right shoulder blade, the one Gaitlin called 'Isla's eider'. She hadn't told him it was done after Manos left.

The videos also featured those who'd set up a temporary camp below their relatives in the park to keep watch, one a stout elderly man who looked like the human incarnation of a grumpy smiley. The Facebook *Let Them Float* group, of which Isla was a member, had 100,000 members so far; there, the man was named as Malcolm Brown, the husband of the second Floater and the person who'd called them 'human balloons'.

She discovered that Mrs Brown was actually the mother of Kylie, the chatty receptionist. At work, she tentatively asked Kylie why her mother might be up there.

'I don't know, Isla.'

'Was anything the matter?'

Wrinkles spread over Kylie's brow. 'Mum retired last year and is at home a lot more. I guess it's been a time of adjustment.'

'Really? I yearn for retirement.' Isla's fingers played with her scarf. 'Keep that a secret from Bev.'

'Don't worry. But how someone feels about retiring depends on their circumstances, doesn't it?'

'Aye. How's your daughter coping, by the way?'

'It's unsettled her a little, but Alice is okay. She sometimes spends time with my dad in the park.'

'Is the wee lass about ten with ginger hair like you? I might have seen her there.'

'Yes, that's probably my darling girl.'

'Your dad's the one who made that human balloon comment, isn't he?'

Kylie's laughter was bubbly. 'Yes.'

On Facebook that evening, Isla discovered that a local musician had produced an electronic track featuring Mr Brown's 'human balloon' comment as a looping sample. As Gaitlin loved such music, Isla played it without explanation. He nodded along enthusiastically until he realised what the words were. 'Not those Floaters again, Isla. Please.'

The following day, Gaitlin suggested they go for a walk in Friday Woods instead of Castle Park. 'Let's avoid the freak show today, eh?' he said.

'They're human beings, not freaks.'

'Yup, because human beings really hang around like weird static birds.'

'Does Mollie think they're freaks, too?'

'I don't know.' He avoided her eye by checking a fingernail.

28

To keep the peace, Isla agreed to go to Friday Woods. It was a pleasant walk, wending through piebald patches of light and shade and pretty carpets of bluebells, but she kept glancing up through the gaps between the tree branches, longing to see glimpses of people there.

Later, slouched on the sofa, Isla and Gaitlin watched two experts debate the Floaters on Anglia News. A bespectacled psychiatrist with a noticeably Roman nose and a public school accent, called Michael Westerly, claimed, 'The Floaters are there because of collective hysteria, perhaps underpinned by emotional dissociation. The individuals may feel unhappy in, or alienated from, their lives, so they become vulnerable to suggestion.'

'But if so, why is it happening here and now?' asked the presenter.

'Mental illness is sometimes mediated by culture. It takes distinct forms at different times. There've been a few scattered incidents of floating in the past, including one in California in 1969, shortly after the first moon landing. Why here and now?' The psychiatrist squinted, as if showing he was considering the question. 'I believe it may relate to all the coverage on social media last month of Milo Owen's trip into space.'

Isla vaguely recalled Facebook posts of the local multimillionaire who'd paid for a place on a spaceship; short videos of him floating in no gravity. She hadn't given them much attention.

'The idea of floating imprinted itself into suggestible minds locally,' said the psychiatrist.

But the other expert, Dr Faiza Asad, a physicist from the university, wasn't convinced. 'Surely the mind isn't powerful enough to defy gravity. I don't know why this is happening, but it's incredibly enigmatic,' she said. 'We need to keep an open mind about the cause and do biochemical tests on the people as soon as they are back to earth.'

'Dr Azad doesn't appreciate the potential seriousness of the situation.' Michael Westerly's chin jutted up. 'I'm concerned the problem will spread.

Tomorrow, I'm going to be lifted on a crane to try to speak to the Floaters, and I'm also recommending that they be tugged back down to earth for their own safety.'

'He's talking sense,' Gaitlin agreed. 'About time someone did something.'

'Really?' Isla twirled her hair around her index finger. Given the Floaters' facial expressions, the psychiatrist might be right about emotional disassociation, but this kind of intervention didn't convince her, and she found Dr Westerly rather pompous. 'Do you think pulling them down is ethical?'

'It's pragmatic.'

'But aren't there questions about consent?'

'Like a top-up?' He pointed to her wine glass.

'No, thanks.'

'I'm going to have one.'

Isla turned up the television volume a little, hoping they'd re-run the footage of Malcolm Brown and his human balloon comment.

***

As Javier planted a kiss on Hope's cheek, Nadine's heart squeezed. Why had Hope invited her, Nadine, to the birthday party? More to the point, why had she agreed to come?

Typical of Javier, the living room had functional furniture and zero personal touches. He stood next to Hope, gawking adoringly at his girlfriend. Did he ever treat Nadine like that? *Well, yeah, before Christos was born*. Actually, he'd told Nadine she was the love of his life after only one month together. That should have been a red flag. Things were just about okay after Gareth arrived, but the second child nuked any romance. After Christos, most of her memories involved Javier's moods, him being arsey in one way or another.

Hope's long, strawberry-blonde hair was dead straight, and her perma-grin marked her out as young and childless. From her mauve short dress came long legs that ended in tottering purple high-heels, and she had a slender, toned body like that

30

of an Instagram yoga instructor. *The cow.* Nadine tugged her baggy cream top down over her size 16 jeans. Why had she worn jeans, anyway?

From the kitchen, someone carried in a chocolate cake – thank god for the chocolate! – rimmed with lit candles, and a gasp sounded through the room. Nadine knew a few people at the party, but most seemed to be Hope's friends, young women with names like Camilla and Venetia. One had told Nadine that she'd attended the private St Mary's School for Girls with Hope. Hardly a surprise – originally from a council estate herself, Nadine had a nose for privilege. She imagined them at school, nattering about ponies over avocado toast. Hope probably grew up in a massive house in the country with stables. *Lucky cow.*

Nadine grudgingly sang along to 'Happy Birthday to You'. Christos joined in, clapping his hands, but Gareth had already bid his retreat to the patio outside, where he sat alone at a table with an iPad.

After Hope had blown out the cake's candles, she said, 'I made a wish,' and smiled flirtatiously at Javier. Nadine watched, feeling dizzy as he kissed Hope on the mouth. No, dizzy wasn't the right word. Her mind, her *self*, seemed to go blank. She drifted outside to the patio and took a deep breath. Did she still have feelings for the sod? Or was it just that his life had moved on while hers hadn't? The warm sun on her face perked her up a little.

'Four Floaters now, Mummy.' Gareth pointed at the iPad.

Nadine ambled over. 'My god.' Her neck tingled as Gareth scrolled through the Facebook photos.

'Cake anyone?' Hope appeared, holding a small plate.

'Me, please,' said Gareth.

Hope put the plate down in front of him, smiling almost manically. 'What's on the iPad, then?'

'Photos of Floaters,' said Gareth.

'Should you be paying that attention, Gareth? A bit weird, isn't it?' This was delivered to Nadine as much as to him.

'Gareth finds it fascinating,' said Nadine.

31

'Like father, like son, then. Javier's intrigued, too.' Hope flicked her long hair with a hand. 'Would you like cake, Nadine?'

'I'll get some.'

'Let me. Please.' She vanished, returning quickly with a plate, which she handed over.

'Ta. Looks good.'

'We're glad you could make it. Javier didn't know if you'd be at the pub today.'

Javier was sniffy about her workplace, and Hope had probably never been to a pub on Greenmore Estate. Nadine imagined them chuckling about her job. 'I only work Friday and Saturday nights there.'

Hope pressed a hand to her chest. 'I have no idea how you cope. I need my weekend time out.'

'I don't have a choice. Are you in the same line of work as Javier?'

'Oh, no. I'm in PR.' Hope's small blue eyes sparkled. 'I'm glad you came today, Nadine.'

'Ta.'

'As I'm going to be spending time with the boys on weekends, I thought it best that we meet properly. So you can see who will be with them.'

'Thanks.' Nadine had to admit that was considerate.

'What do the boys like to do? I talked to Javier and suggested we take them out to the seaside next Sunday.'

'What? He agreed to that?'

'You sound surprised.'

'Well, I'm sure they'd like to go,' Nadine said, trying to backtrack. She glanced at Javier inside the flat. Would he *really* do a seaside trek? Perhaps he was donning the 'perfect boyfriend' act for Hope. Nadine felt sorry for the woman, who surely wasn't aware yet how selfish he could be.

It suddenly occurred to Nadine that she herself was also pretending. Not to impress a new partner, but to keep her boys afloat and happy. As if snared in an eternal audition to be a 'perfect mum'. *Where the hell am I in all this?*

'Are you okay?' Hope stared quizzically.

'Yeah, fine. Ta.'

The music came on inside, the song 'Jump'.

'I have to dance. I adore this track. Catch you later.' Hope slipped indoors.

Nadine checked the time. How long should she politely stay before doing a runner? 'You want to go home?' she asked Gareth, hoping he might offer her an excuse.

'I'm okay.' Eyes glued to the iPad, he ate more cake.

Nadine took a bite of hers. 'Mm, good.' As other people were around, she stopped herself from shovelling the rest down quickly.

Inside, Hope danced with Christos, holding hands with him. Nadine had to give the woman her due for making an effort. Even so, her heart felt steamrolled flat. She was about to look at the Floater photos again when a text arrived from her mum, asking if she and the boys would like to visit during half-term week. Nadine's heart capsized further. That meant a four-hour drive to Wolverhampton and, as her folks lived in a council flat, a cramped, stressful few days. Her dad had been so proud that she was the first in their family to get into university that he'd never quite forgiven her for dropping out. He'd told her it was a mistake. Was he right? Her eyes settled on Gareth. *No. Gareth and Christos exist.* But her dad's judgement still weighed on her like a suitcase of unread books.

On the way home, Nadine took the boys for a brief walk in Castle Park.

'Look! Five now,' said Gareth.

Blimey, they're mounting up. A young lad was up there with four women of various ages. Once in a position, the Floaters didn't move, as though frozen in space. Two women hung just a couple of metres apart above one oak – co-conspirators in floating – while the others were spread out over other trees.

'Do you think there'll soon be loads?' Gareth asked.

'I don't know.'

'Why's there a crane, Mummy?' Christos pointed.

Sure enough, a yellow crane stood near an oak tree, and close to it, on the ground, a metal basket big enough to hold a person. A well-dressed man, with a remarkably beaky nose and little round glasses, talked to a grumpy-looking elderly bloke who kept pointing at a particular Floater. Nadine couldn't hear what was being said.

'I think the one with the glasses is that psychiatrist from the news,' Nadine remembered. 'They said they're going to lift him up to speak to the Floaters.'

'Please let's watch, Mummy,' asked Gareth.

'Let's.' Christos clapped his hands.

The crane slowly lifted the bespectacled man in the metal basket, stopping near the Floater in the blue fleece. He spent some minutes talking to her, but she didn't seem to clock him and carried on staring skyward with that stoned expression. Nadine was secretly delighted.

'What's he saying?' asked Gareth.

'He might be asking why she's up there,' said Nadine. 'Or if she'd like to come down.'

Five minutes later, the psychiatrist returned to the ground, and two men in high-vis jackets ascended in the basket instead.

'Can I have some crisps, Mummy?' Christos swung his arms around.

'No. You only had cake an hour ago.'

Up in the basket, the two men attached a rope to the blue-fleece woman's ankles. She didn't seem to notice, simply hung there like a lemon. They then dropped the rest of the rope down to the ground, where two other workmen picked it up, and the woman, who put up zero resistance, was pulled slowly down to earth. Nadine felt sorry for her. Was this really the right approach?

'But I want her to stay up there,' said Gareth.

'She must be hungry and thirsty,' said Nadine.

34

'Perhaps they eat insects up there, like birds do.' Christos shoved something imaginary in his mouth, pretending to chew. 'Yummy. A fly.' Giggling, he prodded his brother. 'What do you think they eat?'

'Don't poke me.' Gareth nudged his brother, and the two started pushing each other.

'Stop it,' said Nadine firmly, and they obeyed.

Once returned to the ground, the grey-haired woman seemed dazed. The elderly man, his face all crotchety – like a much older Javier – bustled around her. Nadine guessed it was probably her husband. His wife was laid on a stretcher and ferried to an ambulance at the park's edge.

The whole shenanigan was repeated for the lad, but he struggled against being pulled down, flapping his arms like a frantic pigeon trying to flee from a fox. Once back to earth, he also appeared out of it and was whisked away on a stretcher. Nadine's brow furrowed. She hoped the lad might escape later; imagined him thinking, *Sod this,* and sneaking back to the park under cover of darkness to float freely once more.

***

The hospital ward had six beds. Sheila, with a drip in her arm, had been taken there last night and was still asleep today. Malcolm sat on one side of her bed, with Kylie and Alice on the other. Kylie was reading one of those novels she liked, set in Africa or India or somewhere like that.

Alice, in her school uniform and pigtails, held Sheila's hand. 'Is Granny going to be okay?' she asked for the second time.

'Of course, darling,' said Kylie.

Malcolm shifted in his chair, wondering if Sooty was all right; they hadn't had their walk today. He checked the time on his watch. *Give it another hour, then pop back to let Sooty out into the garden.*

'Granny,' Alice exclaimed.

35

'Mum,' said Kylie in the same instant.

Malcolm realised that Sheila's eyelids were open, though her gaze rested on the other side of the room.

'Granny. You're okay.' Alice beamed a smile.

Sheila's eyes shifted slowly to the girl. 'My little munchkin,' she whispered and squeezed Alice's hand.

'Sheila. Thank god.' Malcolm leaned forward.

'Malcolm,' she said flatly, without looking at him.

His lips pursed in annoyance. After all, he'd been sitting here for ages. He wanted to ask why she'd been up there, but not now, and not in front of Kylie and Alice. It'd been the first time in well over forty years that Sheila hadn't been beside him in bed at night. He'd taken hours to get to sleep, grinding his teeth in the dark, and had woken at dawn each morning, worrying if she was okay and when she'd be back.

Kylie hurried off to fetch a nurse.

'Mrs Brown. It's good to see you awake. How are you doing?' said the nurse.

'Um… yes,' said Sheila.

'I'll take your blood pressure.'

Alice moved aside to give the nurse space. He took her blood pressure and pulse. 'All seems fine,' he said. 'We'll be releasing you later today.'

Sheila's brow wrinkled.

'Mum, the doctor earlier said that all your tests came back normal,' Kylie confirmed. 'Well, you were dehydrated and lacking salts, but that's what your drip is for.'

'He said your meta-something had slowed to a snake's pace,' added Alice.

'Metabolism to a snail's pace.' The nurse corrected her gently. 'Anyway, you're definitely on the mend, Mrs Brown, so please eat and drink something.' He pointed to the fruit bowl Kylie had brought. 'Perhaps your family could bring you a cup of tea, too?'

36

While being discharged from the hospital, Sheila stayed quiet. The nurse took Malcolm aside and told him to ensure his wife rested up for a day or so. 'And keep her away from that park,' the nurse said.

'Don't you worry. I will,' he said.

Back home, Sooty went berserk with excitement and wouldn't leave Sheila's side. That his wife was home made Malcolm cheerful, too. He brewed a cuppa and then suggested that she sit in the living room.

'I'd like to get on,' she said.

'Just sit, Sheila, as the nurse advised.'

She did so, frowning. Steam rose from her mug.

Malcolm joined her, in his favourite armchair. 'Nice cuppa, isn't it?' He took a sip. Hot!

Her eyes squinted at the carpet.

'It's good to have you home.' Malcolm put his mug down and fidgeted with his wedding ring. The pressing question burst from his lips: 'Why were you even up there?'

Her gaze settled on her drink and she sipped her tea, saying nothing.

'Sheila?'

'It's....' She replaced her mug on the side table. 'I think it's because... well, Malcolm, I'm not happy.'

He snorted impatiently. 'Why ever not?'

She picked at something on her skirt.

He gestured around the room. 'But we have this house, we have Sooty. You're retired, living a life of leisure. Why unhappy?'

Sheila adjusted her glasses with a finger, staring at the floor.

Later, feeling guilty at his outburst, he told her he'd fix their dinner. For the last week, he'd been getting ready meals from the local Spa, which were tastier than Sheila's nosh. 'I'll pop out to get us cottage pie and peas and an apple pie for pudding. You'll like that.' He wondered if it was wise to leave her alone, but he'd only be five minutes. 'Stay here and rest as the nurse said, Sheila?'

'Yes.'

When he returned, she wasn't in the kitchen or living room, and Sooty whined by the front door. 'Sheila?' *No, not there. Or there.* He rushed around the house a second time, calling her name.

An icy shiver slid down Malcolm's spine. She wouldn't have gone *there,* would she? He put Sooty on a leash and hurried out.

A few grey clouds tainted the blue sky over the park. *Oh Christ, no.* He stared up at Sheila. The others were all back too, in the very same places as before.

***

The Floaters increased quickly in numbers. They featured on the BBC and ITV, and the Facebook *Let Them Float* group that Isla was in now had over 200,000 members nationally.

One day, in Castle Park, Gaitlin said, 'That Michael Westerly has the right idea.' The psychiatrist had proposed pulling all the Floaters down again, strapping them to their beds, and prescribing drugs. But an online petition organised by *Let Them Float* got over 60,000 signatures, and the council bowed to public pressure to do nothing.

'You know I don't agree,' said Isla.

Gaitlin pointed upwards. 'There are well over a dozen, so it'd be good for them at least to *do* something, like play a ball game in the air. Don't you ever get bored watching them?'

'No.' Isla was spellbound – it was akin to a living version of the Magritte painting *Golconda*, which featured numerous people suspended in the sky. Ten Floaters were above trees, the rest in open space.

He frowned. 'Do you think any of them have kids?'

Isla imagined this question was because of Mollie. 'On the Facebook page, it says a few do.'

'Kids need their parents.'

Isla wondered what it took to leave your children in this way.

'Maybe we should get your dad on the case,' said Gaitlin with a wry grin. 'He'd sort them out.'

'Hmm.' Gaitlin often teased Isla about her outspoken dad, who lived in Dumfries. He had no reservations about telling Gaitlin, or anyone else, they were 'talking rubbish', although he appreciated Gaitlin's upbeat nature. Though not close to her parents, Isla still missed her Scottish roots; she'd come south first to study at university and then to work, but her heart was beside the River Nith and Drum Bay.

'Let's get going. I need to marinade the beef,' said Gaitlin.

Isla would have preferred to stay, but couldn't object.

In bed that night, she mentioned how she missed Scotland.

Gaitlin's face was near hers. 'It's great up there. I love the walks and the accent. I sometimes wish yours was stronger.'

Twenty years in England had watered hers down. 'Nae ye dinnae, ye dafty,' she said, putting on her finest Glaswegian.

He smiled. 'Once Mollie's finished at university, we could think about moving up. QTech has an office in Edinburgh where I could try for a transfer.'

Isla glanced away. They hadn't discussed moving in together. She simply avoided the subject, and she suspected fear of rejection meant he'd never brought it up before. That he loved her more than she did him, felt a weight. She was aware of how much heartbreak hurt. But she was concerned about becoming female scaffolding for his male ego, too. 'I don't want to be that far from Hamish.' She checked the clock. 'It's late. Let's go to sleep, eh.' She tucked down, turning the light off.

In the dark, Isla's mind drifted to Manos. Unlike Gaitlin, he'd have been fascinated by the Floaters. Manos was curious about people, having studied social anthropology at the university where he and Isla met. A memory flashed of being with him and his Greek parents at an open-air theatre in Athens. Under a canopy of stars, they enjoyed a performance of Medea by Euripides; she and Manos holding hands, in love, five years after meeting. If Isla hadn't had ovarian cancer, would

39

they still be together? *Stop pining for him. He was a cad for walking out when he did.* Under the duvet, both palms pressed against her womb, empty as an uninhabited shell.

The next evening, a documentary about the Floaters was featured on Channel 4. Relatives and friends were interviewed, talking about how before the floating, there'd been little signs things weren't right – loss of appetite, moodiness. Watching it, Isla shivered and then wolfed down an apple. Her own appetite was excellent.

At work, she noticed her attention drifting, though. She'd find her eyes drawn to the sky outside the window, staring at clouds in the shape of diaphanous whales. In meetings, she'd have to make an effort to follow the latest marketing plan for fig chutney, tempted to say, 'Who gives a flying fig about chutney?' She'd return to her desk and sit there, gazing at the photo of Hamish, twirling a lock of her hair around a finger.

She chatted more with the receptionist, Kylie, whom she liked. 'How's your dad holding up?' Isla asked.

'He seems rather lost without Mum. He spends a lot of time in the park, sitting near her, reading his paper.'

'That's sweet.'

'It'd be even sweeter if it wasn't *The Daily Express*.' Kylie raised her brows.

'I didn't have you pinned as a leftie like me.'

'Dad and I don't see eye to eye on politics.'

'Did your mum ever watch any of those videos of Milo Owen in space, the ones that psychiatrist Westerly said might have influenced people subliminally?'

'I don't know. Mum doesn't use Facebook much. Dad probably did, though. He's got an opinion on everything.'

***

40

Stuck in the traffic jam, Nadine sweated. She was going to be late. She took out a chocolate from her secret stash in the glove compartment and scoffed it. Then another. *Sweets at 8.55 am? Zero self-control!*

At Old Manor, a Georgian house on its own plot, Nadine parked her banger next to the sleek silver Mercedes. Stone steps led up to a white door framed by two stone columns. Mrs Elgar lived here with her husband, something in the City, and two teenage boys. Nadine cleaned for them Monday through Thursday mornings, and on Friday she did the weekly shopping for the family at Waitrose. It had taught her about persimmon fruit and artisan bread and how the other half lived.

Mrs Elgar answered the door. 'You're late.'

'Sorry. Those traffic works are still on London Road. A nightmare.'

A gold necklace complimented Mrs Elgar's elegant olive-green trouser suit. 'Well, you'd better get on. How are Gareth and Christos?'

'Good, ta.' Not true. Gareth had been down since the weekend; Javier having a new girlfriend had upset him.

The marble mantelpiece over the fireplace in the living room collected tons of dust. Thank god Mrs Elgar didn't expect Nadine to fetch a stepladder and polish the chandelier, too. She'd just moved on to dusting the windowsill when the door opened and Bach, the Afghan hound, trotted across. 'Hey, naughty boy. You're not supposed to be in here.' He wagged his tail as Nadine petted him. 'We'd better get you out before your mum finds you.'

As she took hold of his collar, Bach jumped back impishly, thinking it a game. Nadine lost her balance for a second and knocked against a tall glass sculpture of an angel, which tumbled to the parquet floor and smashed. 'Shit,' she exclaimed. Startled, Bach shot out, leaving Nadine to stare in shock at the fragments. The Floaters came suddenly to mind.

Mrs Elgar appeared. 'It sounded like something broke.'

'Sorry. An accident.' As Nadine explained, Mrs Elgar's palm flew to her brow.

'Oh, no. That was one of my grandmother's, an heirloom.'

A spasm of guilt. 'I *am* sorry. Is it insured?'

'I'm not happy about this.'

Immediately before Nadine left the house, Mrs Elgar said she wanted her to pay 'a little something' towards the cost of the broken sculpture. 'I'll just take a hundred pounds from your wages.'

Just? Money was always tight. 'But it was an accident,' Nadine complained. 'If Bach hadn't snuck in, I—'

'That sculpture is worth eight times what I'm asking you to contribute.'

'Is it insured?'

'It was an heirloom, Nadine.'

One thing about cash-in-hand jobs with rich, iron-willed women – it wasn't that easy to protest. A hundred quid meant nothing to Mrs Elgar, but to Nadine...

'I'll dock ten pounds a week for ten weeks,' said Mrs Elgar. 'That'll make things easier, okay?'

'Shit, shit,' muttered Nadine as she drove away. Ten quid was a good chunk of the week's groceries, and she hated asking Javier for extra money. Was there no respite from the crap life bowled at her? Her tummy was playing up too, pain prodding her there. If God existed, he had a 'sod you' finger pointed at Nadine.

She still felt frazzled when she picked up the boys from school. They squabbled in the car, and she snapped at them. In need of fresh air and a walk, she took them to Castle Park, where the scent of freshly mown grass filled her nostrils.

Several weeks had passed since the first Floater appeared. 'How many are there now?' asked Christos.

'Let's count,' said Gareth.

They did. 'Twenty-six. Awesome,' said Christos.

The Floaters all hung in a vertical position. Most were women of various ages, a few were men; some ethnic minorities featured and the majority were white. Some clustered in twos or threes over one tree, and the rest spread out as lone units. Nadine couldn't help but stare.

'Gareth!'

Nadine's attention was drawn to the voice calling. Gareth's friend Hamish waved. He sat on the grass a short distance away with a woman Nadine didn't recognise, not his mum. *So slim, the cow.* Shoulder-length shiny copper hair framed her long thin face. A duck-egg blue neck scarf matched her sundress. *So stylish, too.* Nadine and her boys went over.

'Gareth.' The woman's full lips, beneath a large nose, curled into a half-smile. 'We met at Hamish's party. I'm his Auntie Isla. Remember?' Her voice was tinted with a gentle Scottish accent.

'Yes, I do. This is my brother, Christos, and my mum.' Gareth sounded so grown up introducing them.

'I'm Nadine. You're here watching the Floaters, too?'

'Aye. Hamish and I like to.' Isla's smile held a shadow. 'Care to join us?'

'Okay, ta.' It was good to meet a fellow adult enthusiast in the flesh. Isla and Hamish lay down and stared up, and Nadine and her boys followed suit.

The day was balmy and the grass lightly prickled Nadine's back. For some minutes, nobody talked. Birdsong eddied from the trees. It was rare for her boys to shut up for this long, and knots of tension unwound from her shoulders. She closed her eyes, imagining her body getting lighter, herself drifting up…

'Which was the very first one?'

Christos's voice burst Nadine's fantasy bubble, and she opened her eyes.

'That one.' Hamish pointed it out.

'I say to Hamish that the park looks like a cross between a human balloon factory and a Magritte painting,' said Isla.

Nadine, who got the reference, smiled. 'Yeah.'

'Who's Magritte?' asked Gareth.

'A famous French surrealist painter,' said Isla. 'Dead now, but, like us, he'd have loved the Floaters.'

Christos giggled. 'I want to shoot at them with a giant water pistol.'

'I don't think *they'd* like that,' said Nadine.

'They're people, Christos.' Hamish sat up. 'What's *she* doing, Auntie Isla?'

Sitting up, too, Nadine followed Hamish's pointed finger. A girl of about Gareth's age with ginger pigtails was kneeling some thirty metres away. Twigs were piled by her on the grass, and she seemed to be making something out of them.

Isla said, 'I think she might be the wee daughter of a woman I work with.'

'Come on, Hamish. Let's investigate,' said Gareth. The three boys jumped up and pelted off.

Isla wrapped her arms around her knees. 'I'm so fascinated by the Floaters.'

Nadine was glad to have Isla to herself. 'Yeah. Me too. I feel...' Nadine pondered for a minute, trying to put it into words. 'Well, them being there is weirdly comforting.'

Isla nodded several times and then frowned as if thinking. 'They make me feel less freaky or alone. Does that even make sense?' She sought Nadine's eyes.

'Yeah.' A flash of recognition passed between the women. Isla had nailed it – with the Floaters there, Nadine was somehow less on her own.

'You feel that way even though you have Gareth and Christos?' Isla's fingers worried at her neck scarf.

'I love my kids to pieces, but being a single mum can be isolating.'

'No partner?'

'I'm separated from my husband.'

'I'm sorry.'

'Don't be. I'm not.' Nadine managed a smile.

Isla continued to rub her scarf between thumb and forefinger. 'Sometimes not having kids also makes you lonely.'

'You have none yourself?'

A shadow drifted across Isla's eyes as she shook her head.

'And you're single as well?' asked Nadine.

'I have a boyfriend. He's not keen on the Floaters, though.'

'Relationships can be hard work.'

Isla raised her brows. 'Aye, they can.'

Sudden bland music in the park startled Nadine, probably playing via public speakers. 'What's that?'

Isla grimaced. 'I guess it's the music that psychiatrist mentioned on Anglia News, the one with subliminal suggestions for the Floaters to come down. They're going to broadcast it here for at least an hour every afternoon.'

'They should just leave them be.'

'This music's so rubbish it'll probably drive them down.'

Nadine laughed. She had an urge to reach out and touch Isla's hand in friendship but worried that might freak her out. Isla seemed like the kind of woman Nadine would be happy to hang out with.

***

The music in the park was pleasant. It had no words but apparently carried secret messages for Sheila and the others. *Better do something,* thought Malcolm. He was in his lightweight camping chair, sunblock slathered on his arms and face. Through sunglasses, he stared up at a lone cloud above the Floaters, as if it held the hidden answer to his troubles.

He sighed and looked over at Alice in her pink summer frock and sun hat. She crouched on the grass several yards in front, forming these little twigs she'd picked up into the shape of letters. 'Why not write Granny a message with coloured felt-tip pens on a huge piece of white paper?' he'd suggested yesterday. 'Like a flag. We'll drape it on the grass in the park.' Alice said this way was more 'eco', and Malcolm forced himself not to scoff at that word. 'Got to let Alice do as she wants,' he told Sooty.

A memory suddenly flashed of last night's dream – him driving a black cab in London, frantically lost in the maze of streets. A dream that Malcolm was being plagued by. His punter – a posh bird in a red overcoat – knocked on the glass division and asked, 'Don't you even know the route?' Patronising cow! He'd woken with a start, pulse racing, and taken a minute to remember why Sheila wasn't in bed beside him. He wasn't half missing his wife.

Malcolm shook his head to get rid of the thought and grabbed some sweets from his bag. 'Like a Liquorice Allsorts?' He called loudly enough to be heard over the music.

'No thanks, Grandpa,' Alice called back.

As he ate one himself, his eyes drifted up the park. A couple of nights ago, some anti-Floaters had broken in here during the night and spray-painted on the grass: GET THE BLOODY LOT DOWN. *Good on them.* The council was going to clean the words off, but for now, they remained. Malcolm was onside with that Dr Westerly bloke – Sheila and the others should be tugged down and given drugs to help them snap out of it. The council was being as flaky as ever, but it *had* at least said yes to playing this music.

Three boys of a similar age to Alice were chatting with her. School friends of hers, perhaps. The two Italian-looking ones could be brothers, and the mousy-haired boy in a Chelsea FC t-shirt looked like a good kid. Malcolm wanted to hear what was being said, so he stood up, wincing at his knee pain. The ache eased through the walking.

'I'm making a message for Granny.' Alice's voice could be heard over the music. 'See?'

'Please come down…'The mousy-haired boy spelled out the words so far.

'It's going to say, 'Please come down, Granny. I miss you'.'

'Which is your granny?'

Alice pointed to Sheila above the oak tree.

'What if she likes being up there?' asked the boy.

'She doesn't *look* happy, does she?' said Malcolm. Her expression made her seem completely out of it to him.

'This is my grandpa.' Alice took hold of Malcolm's hand. 'I want to eat apple pie with Granny again. So does Grandpa.'

'Come on, boys. Let her get on,' said Malcolm gently.

The boys bid goodbye and jogged away.

Alice finished the rest of the message, with Malcolm standing over her saying, 'Looks great, my girl,' and, 'I'm sure Granny will love it.'

Just had to hope Sheila would notice the thing. Glancing up at his wife, he thought about that blue balloon again. He frowned, struggling to remember properly. Ah, yes, it was coming back. His mum bought him the balloon to say 'well done' for winning a school running race. In the park, his dad – pissed as a fart, as usual – snatched it off him and let go. Malcolm got upset, but all his dad did was jeer. 'Don't be such a stupid crybaby,' he sneered, his ruddy face close to Malcolm's, whiskey on his stinking breath. Malcolm hated his dad that day; hated the bastard. He longed to be that balloon himself, floating off, and he secretly vowed never to cry again in front of his dad. Never.

Today, the memory brought a tear to Malcolm's eye, and he hadn't cried since their last dog, Fiddler, died a decade ago. *Don't blub when Alice is here, you ridiculous man.* He pretended to be scratching his nose to wipe the tear away.

Up there, Sheila was out of reach. *Don't fly off,* he willed her. *I'm not like my dad... am I?*

***

Isla suspected that the Floaters would all come down of their own free will eventually, and the local council and retail businesses had realised money could be made from the tourist attraction. However, Gaitlin was getting more and more wound up by them. One Saturday, in Castle Park, he moaned, 'A stroll here is like an obstacle course.' Families of the Floaters were gathered, keeping watch over their relatives, and as it was the weekend, Floater Spotters had arrived from around the country.

'But it's almost a festival atmosphere,' said Isla.

'How do they even eat and poo up there?'

47

'I don't think they do.' Isla had read a long discussion about that on Facebook, with scientific and lay theories about how the Floaters survived. The best theory, to her mind, was that each of them hung in their own tiny universe where the laws of physics and biochemistry were suspended. The worst ('they need to fart') held that a dramatic slowing of normal digestion, combined with a large accumulation of gas in the colon, kept the Floaters airborne.

Isla indicated a trinity of women above an oak tree – one young, one middle-aged, and one old. 'Look. It's almost like a holy constellation.'

'It's incomprehensible.' Gaitlin exhaled a breath. 'I'm going to buy those Tuscan sausages with fennel. Coming?'

'Think I'll stay here for a bit.'

'See you back at the flat then,' he said curtly and strode off.

Isla crossed her arms in irritation. It didn't help that some antis then turned up in the park, holding placards: *Floaters R No Hopers, Jesus Doesn't Approve, No To Levitating Zombies.* Some pros with placards appeared, too: *Let Them Float, Jesus Loves Floaters, They Float My Boat.* The two groups stood some way apart, exchanging dirty looks.

She knew friends and colleagues who also had conflict with their loved ones over the Floaters, including Bev, her manager. Bev had told Isla that her in-laws refused to come to Sunday lunch because of their difference in opinion. 'My father-in-law called me a Floater Spotter, whatever that means, and put down the phone,' Bev said. 'I mean, honestly!'

Isla decided it was time to head over to Sainsbury's, but even there she witnessed an argument between two elderly women in the fresh fruit aisle.

'They need to be forced down,' spat one.

'Let them float,' the other barked.

The quarrel built until the first grabbed a packet of runner beans from her trolley. She hurled it at the second, who ducked and shouted, 'You cow!' A mandarin was thrown back. Bam! It landed on the cheek. 'Ouch.'

The first held up a banana, about to chuck it, but a security guard muscled in. 'Put the banana down,' he ordered.

Outside, in the car park, Isla let herself into the car and sat. Her head was spacey; her heart thumped. She pressed her face into her palms. *What's up with me?*

She grabbed her phone, compelled to open it, and seeing the latest Floater photos calmed her, like a soothing bath.

***

'Nadine,' barked Terry, the manager. 'Someone's thrown up in the women's toilets. Deal with it.'

Why did she always get the crappy jobs? It was only just after 8 pm and one wall of a toilet cubicle at The Queen's Head was sprayed with sick. Nadine's gut heaved. *Breathe through your mouth, it lessens the stench.* With plastic gloves on, she cleaned the mess off as quickly as possible.

When Nadine was back behind the bar, Terry – six-feet-five inches tall, with a two-inch battle scar from Iraq on his temple – asked, 'Why've you got the word video on your arm?'

She twisted her arm to show the tattoo on her biceps. 'It's *vida*.'

'*La buena vida*,' said Kieran, another barman, of a similar age to Nadine. A mixed race, stocky chap, with dark eyes wide as a deer's. 'Means 'the good life' in Spanish, doesn't it?'

'I wasn't aware you spoke Spanish,' said Nadine.

'Only some. I worked in a bar in Valencia a few years back.' Kieran had a musical Irish accent.

'Really?'

Terry screwed his nose up. 'That's your grand philosophy, Nadine? Live the good life?'

Not for a long time, she thought.

Terry pointed at a cluttered table where several men drank. 'Grab those glasses, will you, Nadine?'

As she collected the empties, someone patted her on her bottom – a balding bloke with a beer belly. 'Stop that,' she snapped and carried away the glasses. She took Kieran aside to ask if he'd pick up the rest from that table.

'Are the blokes harassing you?' asked Keiran.

'Yeah.'

'Idiots. I'll have a word.'

'Thanks.' Kieran was the coworker she liked the best. It would be pointless to expect Terry to tell punters off.

Nadine left The Queen's Head at midnight, feeling tired after a busy shift. A street lamp cast a pale amber sheen across the pub's largely empty car park. As she reached into her pocket for her car keys, a male voice behind her called out, 'Excuse me, miss.'

Nadine spun tensely around to confront two teenage lads. This area wasn't the safest. One lad had his palm pressed to his eye, as if in pain. She glanced to see if anyone else was around. No one. *Shit.*

'Sorry, miss.' The skinny lad, face blotchy with acne, came closer. 'Some bloke with a knife jumped us. Made us give him our mobiles. Even hit my mate here. Let's borrow your mobile to phone the police?' He held out his palm.

Nadine hesitated. It was unwise to offer her phone.

'Please.' The fat lad still clasped his eye.

'*I'll* phone for you, okay?' She dug in her handbag for her mobile.

The thin lad shot forward, grabbing hold of her bag.

'Let go,' she cried.

A tug of war. She clung on, arms straining.

'Give him the bag.' The fat lad dropped his hand from his eye. In his other hand glinted a knife.

Shit. Her heart hammered, but she held on stubbornly. *I need my phone.*

'Give it to him, you stupid bitch.' He lifted up the knife.

50

My kids! What if I'm stabbed? Nadine let go, her arms slackening, her pulse speeding up further.

'What are you doing?' an Irish voice shouted – Kieran, leaving the pub.

The two lads took off, legged it down the road, and vanished around a bend. Kieran ran over to her.

'They had a knife,' she gasped, pressing a hand to her chest. 'Stole my bag with my phone.'

'Are *you* alright?'

'I guess.' Her heart still raced.

'Were they from the pub?'

'No, youngsters. Didn't recognise them.' Nadine gulped for breath.

'It's okay, you're safe now,' Kieran said gently. 'They might well be caught on CCTV. Do you want to call the police on my phone?'

She nodded. *Shit.* How could she afford a new phone?

After calling to report the crime, she returned Kieran's phone. 'Ta. They want me to go in and make a full statement tomorrow. I should get home now.'

'You should cancel your credit cards, too.'

Nadine never brought her cards to work. 'Oh god, my car keys.' She dug frantically in her coat pockets and felt metal. 'Phew.'

'Want me to drive behind you to ensure you get back safely?'

He had such gorgeous eyes. Part of her wanted to say, 'Yes, yes, please.' Part of her worried about where that might lead.

'I'm not being funny,' he said. 'I just thought you might be anxious about going home alone.'

'It's okay. I'm okay. Thanks for everything.' She offered him a brief wave and hurried to her car.

Inside, Nadine fumbled in the glove compartment for her secret chocolate stash. None left. *Damn.* And how would she receive Facebook updates about the Floaters? She clenched her eyes shut, about to cry. *Don't.* She started the car and shoved it into gear.

Next, she was pulling up in the car park by Castle Park. How on earth had she got here?

Goaded on – the goad invisible but real – she jumped out of the vehicle and found her feet taking her towards the park. *What will the boys do if I bail on them?* The gate was locked at night, but from her teenage years, she knew how to clamber over the old wall at its lowest point. Soon she was alone on the grass.

Beyond the Floaters hovered the full moon, dousing the world with a milky light. How magical! The Floaters were like human Chinese lanterns, haloed by moonlight. Nadine walked forward. Heard something crunch under her shoes – twigs by the looks of it. Possibly the message that the ginger girl had written in twigs. Nadine moved off the spot.

Her eyes were drawn to one Floater. The elderly woman appeared to be coming down slowly from the sky, arms wide to either side. Nadine was unsurprised; it seemed natural. The woman glided down, landed on the grass with a slight bump, and then said with a frown, 'You stood on my Alice's message.'

'I didn't mean to. Sorry.'

'It's nice up there, dear. You look like you should try it.'

As the woman ambled away, Nadine's gaze was tugged to the place above the oak where she'd floated. *So peaceful, so inviting.*

Nadine felt weightless, as if made of oxygen, not flesh and blood; vacant, too, like her brain had switched off. She drifted up and   up.   *Oh,   it's   nice*

better   than

choco   late

***

Malcolm jolted awake. The clock said 1.30 am. He tensed, he sat up. What had woken him? A noise downstairs? A burglar, perhaps? No, Sooty hadn't barked. She did that even at the postman.

He got up. Put his ear to the door. Could hear nothing. From the landing, though, he could see a light downstairs. Was it *her*?

He crept down the stairs, putting his weight more on his right leg, as that took pressure off his left knee. Sooty stood at the bottom, her tail going ten to the dozen. Further down the hallway, he spotted his wife at the kitchen table. 'Sheila,' he gasped.

She was tucking into a large piece of chocolate cake. A half-drunk glass of milk sat beside it. She glanced at him but said nothing. Shoved another chunk of food into her mouth and chewed. Her face was thinner, as if she'd shed pounds. Well, she hadn't eaten in weeks.

'Sheila,' he repeated, sitting down opposite her. As she munched, her chin bobbed up and down. 'Hungry?'

No reply. She finished the cake, then grabbed a banana from the fruit bowl, unwrapped it, and wolfed that down as well. Her eyes remained firmly on the table, avoiding his.

Streaks of bird crap speckled her blue fleece. *Don't mention that.* 'It's good you're back.' Malcolm meant it.

She met his gaze without a smile.

He picked at a button on his pyjamas. 'I said, it's good you're back.'

'Well, Alice missed me.'

'We all missed you.'

Sheila took an apple and bit hard into it.

Malcolm was relieved that she'd returned, but did she need help? 'Shall I phone a doctor?'

Sheila shook her head. After finishing the apple, she let out a yawn.

'You need to sleep?'

She nodded.

She might simply be knackered. Malcolm followed her upstairs. Sheila brushed her teeth, washed her face and armpits, slipped on a nightie, and got under the duvet. She was soon out like a light. Malcolm lay down close to her rank-

53

smelling body. *She doesn't half need a bath.* He listened to her breath, letting its quiet rhythm calm his mind. *My Sheila is home!*

He woke in the morning to find her missing from bed. Worry prodded him, so he quickly got up. He found her downstairs in her dressing gown, drinking tea and staring at Facebook on the computer.

'Morning,' he said. 'Feeling any better?'

She pointed at Facebook. 'People have noticed I'm no longer up there.'

'Oh?'

'Some are saying I was dragged down by the family at night and stuck in an asylum. One woman claims I've floated off into space.'

'What nonsense! Let me see.'

Malcolm read the Facebook posts, his irritation rising. 'I should say something.'

'Tell them to leave me alone.'

He posted from his account: *My wife, Mrs Brown, just had enough. She came down by herself last night without a fuss and doesn't want any bother, thank you very much.*

He let Sheila read it.

'Okay,' she said.

'Need a doctor now?' he asked.

'Why?'

'Well, because of— '

'I'm fine,' she snapped.

'Can I get you anything?'

'I'm going to have a long bath.'

He tried to settle with the paper while she bathed, but couldn't concentrate. Should he call the doctor, anyway?

An hour later, after Sheila reappeared, the doorbell rang. Malcolm opened it to see two men with mics and a crowd of press behind. Their semi was on a side road with little pavement room. He tensed up. 'What do you want?'

54

The younger one asked to talk to his wife.

'No, you can't.'

'Well, I'm afraid we're going nowhere, sir.' The journalist gestured to the press at his rear.

Malcolm shut the door in his face.

'Who was that?' Sheila came out of the kitchen.

As Malcolm explained, a shadow fell over her eyes. 'I don't want to speak to them,' she said.

The doorbell rang again. 'Ignore them,' said Malcolm. 'Go and make yourself a nice cuppa instead.' Then the phone went, some bird from *The Gazette*. How had they got the landline number? Malcolm cut her off.

Half an hour later, the phone rang once more. This time it was Liz from next door, moaning about all the journalists. 'Sorry, Malcolm, but can't you do something?'

After a brief chat, Sheila and Malcolm decided to go outside. Standing close to her, he told the press, 'My wife will answer a few questions, but only if you leave her alone afterwards. Got it?'

'Why were you up there, Mrs Brown?'

Her eyes stayed glued to the ground. 'I don't know exactly. I suppose I... I'd had a hard year and needed...'

A hard year? But she was retired, living the life of Riley. Malcolm knew they often niggled at each other, but that was simply how they were. Was there something he didn't know about?

'Wouldn't a fortnight in Greece have been less dramatic, Mrs Brown?' a reporter called.

Her eyes sought Malcolm, asking for help.

'We hate the sun,' he said. True for him.

'What about the other Floaters, Mrs Brown? You think you set a trend up there?'

'Who knows?' she said.

'Do you imagine they'll all come down too?'

'Perhaps. Is that all? I... don't feel so good.' Sheila's face paled.

Other journalists spoke all at once, but Malcolm said, 'That's enough. My wife needs to rest.'

He shepherded her back inside and shut the door.

***

Isla liked taking Hamish to watch the Floaters, but her sister, Freya, didn't appreciate it.

'Go to the zoo or for a walk instead.' Freya wiped the marble-topped island in her immaculately tidy kitchen. 'Don't you find the Floaters creepy?'

'No, nor does Hamish.' Isla glanced at him. He sat at the far end of the room, near the conservatory, engrossed in his iPad.

Freya stopped cleaning and tutted. 'Hamish. You'd better not be looking at Floater photos on that again. Go and get ready. Now.'

His face flushed as pink as cherry blossoms. 'Okay, Mummy,' he said and left the kitchen.

'Do you have to be so curt with him?' Isla said.

'He's *my* son.'

'He's not a possession.'

Irritation flickered like a toxin in Freya's eyes. 'That's not what I meant.'

Freya always had to have the last word. The two of them were never close, even as kids. The four-year age gap hadn't helped, nor had the fact that Freya was the no-self-doubt, straight-A sister at school, while Isla, more reserved and unsure of herself, struggled to achieve Bs. Their dad used to boast to his friends about Freya, rarely about Isla, which had upset her. She felt in Freya's shadow even when she got a place to study Sociology at Essex University (Freya studied Law at Cambridge), and Isla was initially disappointed when Freya announced, a decade ago, that she, her husband, and baby Hamish intended to move from London to this

56

town, as they could afford a big property here. But Isla was happier and more confident then anyway, living with Manos.

These days, Isla sometimes felt the second-rate sister again, like the sting of cold stone under barefoot. Why did Freya even get to be the top dog where having children was concerned? *I'd be a good mum to a lovely wee lad like Hamish.*

In the car, Hamish and Isla agreed to go to Castle Park. 'You won't tell Mummy, will you?'

'No. It's our secret. I'll pretend we visited Highwoods.'

At the park, she said, 'Tell me what intrigues you so much about the Floaters.'

'They're like sad angels, only without the wings or halos.'

'Remember those Hornies? You admired them, too.' Little goat-like horns had appeared for months on some teenagers' heads and then vanished out of the blue.

'They were awesome.' He pointed a finger. 'See there? More fangirls.' Two young women were in denim. Floater fangirls had become a thing, each dressing in the manner of a particular Floater.

'Oh, yes.'

'And look right over there, Auntie Isla. Doesn't that new Floater seem a little like Gareth's mummy?' Hamish pointed again.

The Floater was a way off but had the correct body shape and hair. Nadine was voluptuous, not skinny and flat-chested as Isla herself. 'Let's go closer.'

She'd first met Nadine in the park while observing the Floaters. The woman seemed overwrought, as if life happened too hard and fast to her and she didn't know how to stop it. The two of them became friends on Facebook, and it was Nadine's striking aquamarine eyes that Isla recalled the most.

As the Floater came clearly into view, Hamish's mouth dropped open. 'It *is* her, isn't it?'

'Aye.' Isla was surprised too, as Nadine appeared devoted to her kids.

'Do you think Gareth knows?' asked Hamish.

57

'No idea. Does his daddy live in town?'

'Yes. Gareth's at his daddy's today. I'll send him a message later.'

'It's better to wait and see if Mummy can contact his daddy somehow and let them know that way.'

Isla wondered why Nadine was up there. And also *how*. Occasionally, when in the park alone, Isla would close her eyes and will herself to float up, but nothing ever happened, gravity her inexorable tether.

Whenever Isla dropped Hamish off after taking him out, her spirits dropped. But today, on arriving home on her own, she sensed something else, too. It was as if a subtle gap had levered open between her and the world – although she wasn't hallucinating or anything like that. She tried to focus on the false acacia tree at the edge of the communal car park. Did it – or she – seem to be fading a little out of existence? She blinked.

The sensation continued that week, a vague pall hazing over her mind. She coped fine with the basics: attended work; saw Gaitlin; watched Hamish play rounders for his school team; and chatted with friends on the phone. But she'd become a self she no longer understood, drifting through an environment she didn't fully recognise; a small grey cloud within a large fuzzy sky. She tried to shake herself out of this state; she started swimming at the pool. Gaitlin offered to accompany her, but she preferred to go alone. Even when the feeling dissipated for a day or so, though, it promptly reemerged. Everything seemed unreal and ungrounded.

On her 41st birthday, she had friends and her sister's family over to the flat. Gaitlin, whose idea the party was, had spent the entire week preparing food. The table brimmed with mouth-watering dishes, among them a tower of chocolate profiteroles and a pink iced cake shaped like a seahorse. Isla chatted and smiled, pretending to have fun while feeling lost inside, as if giving a poor performance in an amateur dramatic theatre of life. She retreated to the bathroom to stare in the mirror. At the bob dyed the colour of new pennies, and the crow's feet gathered at the corners of the small eyes. *Who is this?*

58

The dark red of her lipstick drew her gaze. *Like blood.* Memories cascaded back of bleeding in her knickers at the wrong time. Not her period. Twice it heralded a miscarriage, once the ovarian cancer that preceded her hysterectomy. She gazed at the stranger in the mirror – herself. *I can't have my own kids.* Grief pushed at her throat and she flipped the lid down on the toilet, slumping to sit. Tears blurred her vision.

Sudden laughter jolted her awareness back to the party. *Oh, pull yourself together!* She wiped her eyes and touched up her makeup.

Her brother-in-law, Ian, stood waiting for the bathroom in the narrow hallway outside. 'Good party,' he said.

'Thanks.' Isla forced a smile.

'The cake is delicious. It must be nice to have Gaitlin as your private chef.'

'Yes,' she said through gritted teeth. Ian and her sister often made a point of complimenting Gaitlin in some way. Isla thought they preferred him to Manos because he was wealthier and shared their Conservative views. She slunk past Ian. 'Excuse me. I need another drink.'

***

o   mmm   o

mmmmm

ahhhhh   o   crow

'Mummy!'

'Nadine! The boys are here, below you. Look down!'

'Mummy!'

59

o   *mmmmmm*
aa   *ahhhhh*   *o*

'Caw   caw.'

'Mummy! Mummy!'

ee   *o*   *ahhhh*   *mmmmmmm*
              o   *crow*

'Caw   caw caw caw.'

'Mummy! Come down.'

o   *mmmmmm*
ah   *ahhhh*   *o*

'Pleeeeeeease, Mummy.'

***

Peeking from behind the drawn curtains, Malcolm noticed the press outside again. Not as many as yesterday, but enough to clutter up the pavement and stress him. *Damn journalists.*

He was worried about Sheila. She'd hardly spoken since she got back and seemed busy with her own thoughts. Well, she'd taken a phone call from Kylie and yakked on for an hour in another room, but apart from that, she'd sat in the kitchen, knitting a scarf for Alice. *Click click click,* went the needles. The turquoise and bright pink wool, Alice's favourite colours, spooled on the table. *Click, click, click.*

'Fancy a cuppa?' Malcolm asked her.

'What? Another?'

She'd had this lippy attitude since returning, which was unlike her. How to get his head around it? He sat down opposite her at the table. 'We should book you an appointment with the doctor,' he said.

The needles fell quiet as she looked at him. 'Why?'

'Something's wrong.'

'Well, there *is* something wrong, but...'

'But?'

'I don't need a doctor, Malcolm.' She put her knitting down and a tear spilled from her eye.

He reached to take her hand, unusual for him. 'Everything's okay. Don't you worry.'

Sheila pulled her hand away. 'It's not, though, is it?'

'What?'

'The problem's... us.' Her face said, 'There, I've told you.'

His lips pursed. 'Us?'

'I... I'm unhappy, Malcolm, and I have been for some time.'

He knew things hadn't been perfect for years. Happy once, they'd grown apart. Sheila enjoyed spending hours with her friends, nattering on; he'd become antisocial, preferring to watch football or be with the dog. He got angry about the

61

state of the world; she didn't seem to give a monkey's. But they'd muddled through in their own way. They were Malcolm and Sheila, part of each other, peas in the same pod. 'Come on, Sheila. You're just stressed.'

She shook her head. 'It's more than that. Kylie has been pressing me to talk to you for ages, but it's hard. We... never talk properly about anything.' Another tear slid down her cheek, and she wiped it with a finger.

Words then poured from her like water from a tap left on, telling him all the ways he upset her: he didn't notice when she'd had her hair done or put on nice clothes... didn't value her cooking... seemed to care more for the dog than for her... was closed-minded, a bigot.... could be critical of Kylie, whom Sheila was proud of...

Eventually, she stopped.

Malcolm just stared. He knew he wasn't the easiest man, but was he as awful as she made out? Or had anything happened to her brain up there, floating like that?

'Well, say something,' she said.

'I... I missed you a lot,' he heard himself say. Uncommon words for him.

'You did?'

Malcolm nodded several times.

The doorbell rang, the distraction a relief. 'Probably those journalists again,' he said.

'Oh, no.'

He didn't answer the door but from the window saw it *was* the press. An idea came. 'Let's get away together for a few days. Drive up to that place in Norfolk.'

'No. I'll go and stay with Kylie for a bit.'

'But the press will follow you there. Think of Alice.'

'Kylie will handle the press.'

'But it's obvious *you're* stressed by them, and it isn't fair to Alice. Let's do a runner up to Norfolk. We can talk more there if you like.' She was always happy in the cafes and on the beaches. In truth, he hoped they could forget about her words there. Tidy them away in a box. Put a lid on them, so they meant nothing.

'I... I'm not sure.'

The landline rang. Malcolm answered it and took a message from the hospital. On replacing the receiver, he said, 'That psychiatrist, Michael Westerly, wants to have a talk with you in person this week.'

'Who?'

'The expert. The one on the crane who chatted to you when you were up there.'

Sheila screwed up her nose. 'What does *he* want?'

'To talk about what happened.'

She considered it for a moment. 'I'd rather go to Norfolk.'

'Let's shoot off tonight, then.'

'How will we get past the press?'

'We'll sneak off at midnight or whenever they've gone home. I'll phone the Sandcliff Guest House and book. I'm sure Liz would look after Sooty for a few days.'

'Okay.'

***

For the seventh day in a row, Isla woke at 3 am with adrenaline scouring her like a whip driving a horse. She lay in the dark, rubbing her temples with a finger. She turned onto her side. Shut her eyes. Tried not to listen to the distant hum of traffic. No good. Sleep refused to come.

She got up and ate a banana. Carbohydrates were comforting. She hovered by the shelves, staring at her seahorse collection, the wee animals made of glass, ceramic, and wood, in pinks, oranges, turquoises. 'What's wrong with me, Pygmies?'

Did she expect an answer?

Her disquiet prompted more questions. Should she try to find another job, despite her past efforts coming to nothing? Her eyes settled on the orange Pygmy 21, the gift from Gaitlin. Perhaps she should end things with him? Would that improve her life? She enjoyed the sex – apart from his tendency afterwards to ramble about the problems in Ipswich Town FC's midfield. The relationship took the edge off how isolated she felt, even if it left her ultimately lonely. It was like a muffin with tasty icing, despite the cake being somewhat stale. But was she gutless in staying with him? How badly would she smash his heart if they broke up? The thought of trying internet dating again filled her with dread – a roller coaster without the thrills.

Isla let out a long breath. Life was unfathomable. Or she was inadvertently missing those moments when its nature somehow became fathomable.

She returned to bed but couldn't get back to sleep, so she opened Facebook on her phone. Her heart dipped as she read posts indicating that four Floaters had come down, including Nadine, it seemed. There were Facebook theories:

The subliminal messaging in that music is working.
Isn't it only the women with kids? The blokes are all still up there!!
Perhaps they just needed a sandwich and a dump, lol :)

I don't want the Floaters to vanish, thought Isla. At least Gareth and Christos had their mum back, however. She sent a Facebook message to Nadine: *Hope you are okay x*

The next day, exhausted and fraught, Isla mentioned to Gaitlin that she was having sleeping problems.

'Oh?' he said distractedly, turning on the television to watch Bake Off.

She wanted to shake him by the shoulders.

Isla divulged that she'd been half an hour late for work that morning after stopping to gaze up at the Floaters. 'Bev actually told me off.' It was a mistake to say anything, her tiredness making her careless.

'You should stop going to the park altogether.'

'Why would I do that?'

'You're becoming addicted, for Christ's sake.' His voice rose in volume.

'Don't be ridiculous.' She strode out of the flat, slamming the door behind her, and ran down the stairwell. In the communal car park, lit by a street lamp, she slumped down on the curb and burst into tears, burying her face in her hands.

'Isla!' Gaitlin followed her out. 'Look. I'm sorry.' He crouched beside her. 'Are you okay?'

'No.' Her shoulders shook as she cried.

'Come here.'

Isla let him gather her to him; his hug was comforting. The tears dried up, and she wiped her snotty nose with a hand.

Gaitlin produced a tissue from his pocket and handed it over. 'Feeling better?'

She blew her nose. 'Aye, thanks.' He was rarely emotionally supportive. It made a difference when he was.

'I'm worried about you.'

'I...' What *was* so wrong? 'I've just been sleeping so badly.'

'It'll be okay.'

Isla took his hand and squeezed it affectionately.

He kissed her gently on the cheek. 'Let's go in.'

***

At the school gates, a couple of mums whom Nadine knew didn't raise their hands to greet her. She wanted to say, 'Yeah, I know I lost the plot. I didn't mean to and I'm back quickly, aren't I?' But what was the point?

On Facebook, it was the female Floaters with kids, like her, getting the most hate. In the comments, she'd been called a lazy bitch and a negligent mother, which had made her want to write *enough with the judgement already!* Thankfully, a few people, including that cool Isla, had contacted her to ask if she was okay.

Gareth and Christos tore down the path and clung to her. 'Mummy. You're back,' they cried.

Nadine hugged them for a time, her heart ballooning with affection. 'It's good to see you,' she said. 'I'm so sorry. I love you both very much.'

As she opened the car door for the kids, the question returned: what drove her up there? The shock of being mugged or something more? She rubbed her temples. Javier had told her that, during the five days she was in the air, he accompanied the kids to the park multiple times, and they shouted up. Was that what compelled her down to earth? She couldn't remember the time apart from the crow perching on her shoulder. It was like her brain had been put on mute there, or like her memories had been scooped out when she returned.

A holiday from reality.

Today, when Nadine arrived home with the boys, the normally quiet road was filled with a dozen members of the press. *Oh, shit.* As she parked up, one journalist spotted her. The others promptly swarmed towards her, making her stomach churn. 'Stay in the car for now,' she told the boys and got out alone.

'Nadine. Why were you up there?'

'Nadine. What did it feel like?'

Her hand shielded her face. 'I need to get my kids inside.'

'Two other Floaters also came down last night, Nadine. Did you talk to them?'

'No.' The first thing she remembered was finding herself by her car in the car park, craving a drink of water.

'Nadine. Is the floating coming to an end?'

'I have to get my kids indoors.'

'But Nadine—'

Anger flared in her. 'Let me through.'

'Let her,' commanded one man.

The press stepped back, making space for the boys to leave the car. She herded them inside and locked the front door. 'Don't open it to anyone,' Nadine told them. She drew the curtains in the living room. They were an ugly brown material, fraying at the edges; the landlord had said no to her request to change them. The journalists wouldn't get a close-up shot of them, would they? Sneer about the state of her house?

The boys, who were subdued, clung to her. Nadine offered cuddles, cooked their favourite tea – pasta with fried bacon, cheese, sweetcorn, carrots and peas – and gave them a chocolate dessert. She also ate one herself.

Relief swept through her when the press finally left around 7.30 pm. She tucked the boys up in bed, telling them she loved them. Then she slipped downstairs and guzzled too many chocolates.

She had the strength of mind to avoid Facebook, even though she possessed a new phone – well, Hope's old one, an iPhone 9, worth more than the stolen android. Hope was kind to have sorted this out within a day. Nadine had to admit she liked the woman.

Shattered, Nadine retired to bed early but lay agitated and awake in the dark. Her stomach was bloated, so she rubbed it. She turned over and over again. She sighed. *Nothing's really changed.* It still seemed like she was zooming alone down a B-road, a passenger in a car with no driver. Eventually, she took two herbal sleeping pills to get off.

Thank god the press didn't doorstep her on Friday, perhaps because of the kids. But both boys played up when she dropped them off at Javier's.

'Please don't leave us again, Mummy.' Gareth held on tight to her.

'I won't, my love.' Nadine stroked his hair. 'I'll phone you tomorrow. Promise.'

It was a hectic night at work; awkward, too. After downing a few beers, Bill Turner, a regular, asked her what it'd been like up there.

'I don't remember.'

'Were you filled up with gas?'

'Pardon?'

'That's my theory. Too much gas inside keeps the Floaters up there.' He made a loud, farting noise with his lips and cackled. His friends chuckled, too.

'Leave her be, Bill,' said Kieran.

Nadine's cheeks reddened. 'Honestly, it's no big deal,' she lied. She wouldn't have come to work unless she needed the money.

When the shift ended, Kieran offered to walk her to her car. The police hadn't caught the muggers, who were still at large.

Outside the pub, in the lamplight, Kieran's skin glowed, as if daubed with luminous paint. 'Are you really all right after everything?' he asked.

How kind he'd been tonight. Well, he always was. 'Don't worry,' she said.

His eyes tried to read her face. 'I'm not sure you are okay.'

He was right. Anxiety was setting her on edge. Left to her own devices during the day tomorrow, might she end up above the park again, bailing on her boys despite herself? Would they forgive her a second time? 'You don't fancy going for lunch or a walk tomorrow?' she said.

His grin revealed dimples. 'Are you asking me out, Nadine?'

Heat flushed through her. She didn't want to be alone, but the thought of dating Kieran set her heart racing, too. 'If I was, what would you say?'

'Oh, come on, Nadine. You must know I like you.'

'You do?'

'Ever since we first spoke, I've been summoning the courage to ask you out.'

'You have?'

'You're beautiful.'

The words conjured a smile from her. Then came a flash of worry. 'You don't mind that I've got kids?' He had none himself.

When he grinned, his eyes shone. 'Gareth and Christos sound like great kids.'

In the car, Nadine had no desire to reach for the chocolates. She drove off, excitement pressing at her chest. *He's gorgeous.* How come she'd never sussed that

68

he liked *her*? She couldn't stop smiling as a vision flew to her of them walking hand in hand through the Barcelona streets.

***

To the right, the pier stretched into a sea the grey of Malcolm's Peugeot. The sun shone brightly, and the sky was a clear blue. A Tuesday in term-time meant that few people were around, thankfully. Malcolm wasn't a fan of crowds.

They sat on a bench, having been in Norfolk for over a day. The drive up had been quite the thrill. They'd arrived at four in the morning and waited hours for the hotel to open, huddling in the car, drinking coffee from a thermos and noshing on biscuits, like two runaway kids. But since then, Sheila's mind seemed to have been elsewhere. All those things she'd said – well, they hovered around him like a fog.

'Nice here,' Malcolm said.

'Mm.' She stared out to sea.

'Shall we wander along to the pier? Get one of those ice creams?'

'I think we should talk.'

His heart squeezed. He'd hoped she wouldn't bring up that worrying stuff again. 'You said a lot the other day.'

'Did any of it go in?'

He itched his neck in irritation. 'I worked hard all my whole life to provide us with a good home and food on the table.' Malcolm recalled sorting rubbish at a tip, the job he'd started at sixteen, long before the days of Health and Safety. His dad, always at the boozer, was a waste of space, so Malcolm had needed to work from an early age.

'I know you did.' Sheila scratched her nose. 'But there's more to a marriage than that, isn't there?'

He shifted in his seat. What should – could – he say?

'What I want to know is, how ready are you to try to change?' she said.

69

'Don't you love me as I am? Isn't marriage about accepting the person, warts and all?'

'That works both ways. I… I've tried for many years to accept who you are. It's not that easy.'

Malcolm was aware he could be grumpy and difficult.

'You never listen to me or Kylie,' she said.

'Did she put you up to this?'

'Nobody put me up to this. She's the one telling me to talk to you. She loves how you are with Alice. You obviously adore that girl.' Sheila's tone changed, as if it was frayed at the edges. 'Why can't you be the same with me?'

He fiddled with his wedding ring, unsure how to reply. He *was* more doting with Alice than with anyone, but he'd never imagined Sheila might take it so personally.

'I'm going for a walk on my own, which will give you time to think. Let's meet at the chippy at 6pm,' she said.

'No, don't walk away,' he wanted to say, but his pride gagged him. He watched her stride off, tasting the acid bile of anger rise in his throat. She wasn't the wife he recognised. He stood up and took off in the opposite direction, striding briskly. His left knee hurt, but what the hell!

On the wind farm off the coast, the turbine sails sped round and round. Malcolm stopped, the spinning drawing him in. Panic rose within him, and he pressed a palm to his brow, trying to get a handle on the feeling. It was like life's inner motor had snapped, like everything was wheeling out of control. How would he cope without Sheila? How? She'd been there every day since he was twenty. Every damn day. Was she right that he hadn't been a good husband? The thought made him wince with guilt.

'Are you okay?' A white-haired lady, hunched over a cane, stared at him.

'I'm fine,' he said, although he didn't believe that. He lowered his gaze and strode on. Walked and walked.

Malcolm nearly stumbled over a small toy toucan lying on the promenade. He was tempted to stick a boot into it, but made himself pick it up instead. Perhaps it was a sign. Sheila adored those birds and had a few as ornaments. As the memory of St Andrew's church on their wedding day suddenly flooded back, a tear stung his eye. He recalled how pretty and alive Sheila had looked in her white lace dress, already pregnant. His heart had been ready to burst because she was everything he ever wanted. *I still love the woman. I do.*

At 5.56 pm, he was at the chippy, checking his phone every minute. Sheila arrived at 6.04 pm and nodded hello. 'The usual?' he asked.

'Please.'

Malcolm ordered two cod and chips with salt and vinegar.

They perched on the same bench as earlier, not talking. He bolted his grub down, not tasting it. He then took both their rubbish to a nearby bin. His fingers were sticky with grease and, back at the bench, Sheila handed him a tissue to clean them.

Malcolm fetched the little toucan from his pocket. 'I found this for you.'

Sheila took it. 'I like toucans.'

'Yes.'

'They're not good at flying,' she said quietly.

Malcolm's gaze dropped to his knees. 'I've never been a bloke who wears his heart on his sleeve, but I do love you, Sheila.'

The toucan stopped turning in Sheila's fingers. 'What? More than Sooty?'

Was she joking? He couldn't tell from looking into her eyes, but he *did* love them both in different ways. Diplomacy was called for. 'Of course.'

'I'm not sure words are enough anymore.'

'I... I don't know how I'd cope without you.' Words hard to say.

Her eyes grew in surprise and then settled on the sea in the distance. 'But what about me? I can't cope with our marriage as it is.'

'What's brought all this on? What happened up there?'

71

'I remember little except for feeling… freer, easier. It transformed me somehow. I've realised something must change.'

Change, a word that made Malcolm sweat. 'But is there hope for *us*?'

She considered it for a minute. 'If you want to stay together, the only way forward is to try couples' counselling.'

Counselling was for the crazies, wasn't it? Malcolm's urge was to shake his head no, but the wilful look in Sheila's eyes stopped him. Her lips quivered as if she were readying for a spat. 'Counselling?' he said.

'Yes, counselling. Anne attended with her hubby for a year, remember? I'm not making any promises, but if you're willing to make a big effort, we might have a chance.'

'What do you even do in counselling?'

'You talk and you listen. That'll be the hard part for you – listening.'

Losing her for a time to the Floaters had made Malcolm realise what she meant to him. He knew he couldn't bear to be without her. But the words that fell from his mouth still surprised him: 'Okay, then. I'll do it for you.'

***

'What's the occasion?' Isla asked in surprise as they drew up in the taxi outside Le Torfette, Gaitlin's favourite restaurant. He'd texted earlier to say he was taking her out for a meal on him, so she'd assumed a quick curry. Because of the price, they only came here on special occasions, and they normally went Dutch.

'Can't I spoil my girlfriend now and then?'

'Aye, I guess. I'm underdressed, though.' She glanced down at her lilac tunic top and jeans; he wore a suit and tie.

'You look fine.'

Since Isla's outburst in the car park, things had been easier between them, even if tensions over the Floaters remained. She was less spacey and sleeping much better, too. Life's tribulations had dialled back towards Bog-Standard Frustration. He might be celebrating that.

Oak beams adorned the ceiling of the restaurant, while the candlelit tables, crisp white tablecloths and polished silver cutlery were accompanied by a violin concerto playing tastefully in the background. If the restaurant were a person, thought Isla, it'd own a pearl necklace and a Gucci bag. She felt a fraud here, in the kind of place her sister frequented. She and Gaitlin ordered food, and he selected a £68 bottle of wine.

'It's obscene to spend that much on booze,' she said.

'Do you always have to be such a leftie?' As ever, Gaitlin's relaxed smile carved years off him. 'We'll have that bottle, please,' he told the waiter.

Isla noticed he wore his antique Victorian gold cufflinks, the ones inherited from his father and engraved with a *fleur de lis*. Why?

During the main dish, Gaitlin asked, 'How's the fish?'

'Aye, food of the gods.'

After a delicious dessert of pear pavlova, Isla popped to the toilet and retouched her lipstick. Her mind flicked to later. Even though it was a weekday, they'd have sex after this.

Back at the table, Gaitlin stared at his phone.

'Checking the Floater photos again?' she joked.

'Look at this.' He handed her the phone.

The *Rightmove* app was open, showing a property in Albert Road, two streets away from her flat. All newly refurbished, three bedrooms. Isla's skin prickled. 'And?'

'Well, your flat's so convenient for your work, but there's obviously no spare room for Mollie. I'm considering selling my house and buying something like this.' Gaitlin lived on the other side of town.

Her shoulders tensed as she realised what this night might be about. 'So… we're nearer to each other?'

'Actually, I thought you could move in with me.' His pupils dilated.

73

Isla's heart shrank. She dipped her line of sight so he wouldn't see her expression. He'd misread her, and now she had no choice but to break the poor man's heart. The phone in her hand told her it was nearly eleven o'clock, offering a weak excuse. 'Sorry. It's much later than I thought, and I'm tired. Let's get the bill and talk about it another time, okay?'

'Okay,' Gaitlin said in a hushed tone.

In the taxi, a tense silence sat between them, the awkwardness like a pebble in a shoe. When they pulled up at her flat, he said, 'I'm actually not going to stay over. I've got a hectic day tomorrow.'

Guilt slid through her. 'Thanks for the lovely meal.'

He gave her a kiss on the cheek before she got out.

Inside, as Isla played an LP by Everything but the Girl, numbness slowly percolated her like a mist descending on the back lane of existence. Reluctantly, she'd finish with Gaitlin this weekend, which meant a tunnel of loneliness or stressful dating ahead. Her future seemed shut off from possibilities, yet her past was equally empty. She stared at her hands – well, they were supposed to belong to her. *Someone's pretending to be me, someone dressed in my skin.* She wondered if the reality of things was an illusion.

Insomnia visited her later, with a vengeance.

The next day, instead of heading home after work, Isla went to The Castle pub. Had a glass of wine. Then another.

Somewhat drunk, she wandered into Castle Park. Mackerel clouds stretched across the early evening sky, and there were far fewer human balloons than a week ago. No one knew why they were coming down in dribs and drabs, perhaps because of that annoying music.

Isla stared up. *Let me float.*

Suddenly, it was as if gravity was switched off. A curious sensation followed, like her veins ballooning with air. She took off and floated up. It wasn't exhilarating, more a sense of release. Buoyed rather than overjoyed.

74

no cares
air envelops me
holds me in gaseous sea
breezes freely brush my skin
gulls glide by on wings
up here up high
in the sky
f
l
o
a
t
i
n
g

The Rabbits of the Apocalypse

'How come they're huge?' said Luza.

'Who knows?' Three rabbits, each well over half a metre tall, were nibbling the grass on the crest of Greenacres Hill. We and other passersby stopped to gawk, but the white furred animals were oblivious.

'I wonder where they've come from,' said Luza.

'Who knows?' I said.

She fixed me with her dark eyes. 'You're doing it again, Soph.'

It bugged her whenever I answered her questions with questions. I shrugged.

It was an overcast day and, when a light rain started, the rabbits hopped over to an oak tree to shelter. Two children approached the huddling animals. 'Here, bunny, bunny,' they called.

The animals hunched closer, one squeaking in fright.

Shivering, Luza zipped up her black faux-leather jacket; badges saying *Eco Worrier* and *Lettuce All Be Vegan* were pinned to its front. She pulled her beanie hat further down over her dyed pink hair. 'Maybe they need rabbit umbrellas.' As Luza grinned, the tiny gap between her front teeth showed.

'You could knit them bunny ear muffs.'

'Or make them rabbit raincoats from PVC.' Luza was a whizz at all crafts.

The rain fell harder. I opened my umbrella and stood next to Luza on her mobility scooter so we could both take cover.

***

76

Two days later, there were eight rabbits on Greenacres Hill. The trio were joined by three greys and two white ones with black patches. A few of the newbies looked like youngsters, the others were adults and as large as the originals.

'Think they've escaped from somewhere?' said Luza.

Who knows? Maybe jumbo rabbits are just one of life's mysteries, I considered saying but didn't. The difference between us was that she always wanted to know *why,* whereas I accepted – perhaps from my work as a radiographer – that life threw up oddities. For donkey's years, Luza and I had known each other's foibles too well

Word had spread quickly through town about the rabbits, and we were part of a crowd. Kids particularly loved being near them. Two little girls in school uniforms and pigtails approached them with carrot batons, which they crept up to accept and then scurried away to eat. They were getting friendlier.

***

The next Saturday, there were about two dozen. It was a chilly April day, and they were clustered together in a duvet of fur.

'How odd.' Luza told me she'd been having dreams about the rabbits, and last night she'd dreamt of a hundred, forming a kind of furry pond. 'I was struggling to keep afloat above them, in this little boat made from newspaper, rubber ducks, and Sellotape.'

'Your dreams are weird.'

'Tell me about it.'

It started to rain lightly. I'd forgotten my umbrella.

'Let's get home.' Luza grimaced.

'Are you in pain?'

'My thighs are bad today.'

It wasn't easy for her, having severe fibromyalgia, especially when the rest of our twenty-something friends had busy, active lives. Once or twice a week, I

77

dropped in to see her or we met here on the hill, but she couldn't go out often or stay out long.

***

A fortnight later, there were well over a hundred rabbits.

'Your dream was true.' I stared in awe.

'You don't think I've become a kind of weird rabbit prophet?'

'Or a bunny oracle. Perhaps.'

The rabbits had grown bolder, hopping up to passing kids to see if they had carrots or snacks, or sniffing at inquisitive dogs. One group of ten was dozing, and a child was curled up with them, his eyes closed.

'I'd like to sleep with the rabbits, too,' said Luza.

'If you do, mind the poo.' That was the size and shape of large marbles. There was a lot of it, and a couple of blokes from the council came regularly to clear it off the grass.

The rabbits were attracting the local religious cranks, too. About fifteen metres away, a sour-faced man in a parka held a sign: *These are the Rabbits of the Apocalypse.*

I pointed out the sign to Luza, laughing.

'You don't think he might just have a point?' On her thin face, her brow was creased.

'Don't be daft.'

'I'm not saying it's the end of the world or anything, but maybe these rabbits have appeared because we're out of balance with nature.'

'The rabbit apocalypse. Jesus.' I couldn't help but laugh again.

The man, who must have overheard, shot me a dirty look.

Luza stared at the animals. 'I've heard rumours that the council is thinking of doing something drastic.'

'Like what?'

78

'Dunno. They'd better not hurt them.'

Luza then told me her latest dream: 'All the rabbits invaded the cinema and lived there as old documentaries about nature played in the background on decomposing screens.'

***

Another week later, all the rabbits had disappeared except three, which were found cowering under a bush on Greenacres Hill. However many carrot sticks they were offered, the trio refused to budge.

I'd heard a rumour at work that they'd been herded into a lorry during the night and taken away, to end up as pet food. I told Luza this.

'Jesus. If that's true, I'll nuke the council,' she said.

'You have nukes now?'

'Yes, in the kitchen cupboard next to the Hobnobs. '

A child started crying inconsolably. 'Where are the rabbits? Where are the rabbits?'

He wasn't the only one unsettled. For the next few days, I saw people standing on Greenacres Hill, staring into space, at something they wished were there.

***

The following Sunday, ten rabbits, four of them youngsters, had reappeared and were nibbling the grass. My heart pulsed with excitement.

'Cool! They're back,' said Luza.

They were wary of people now, scuttling away when children approached. One even growled a little when a man walked up to it. Luza told me how some animal rights activists she knew intended to keep watch at night, to ensure the animals didn't vanish again. 'These rabbits are important somehow. Meaningful.'

Maybe she had a point, but what was the meaning of bunnies?

***

The rabbits multiplied quickly. Soon there were twenty, then forty, then too many to count. Various colours and sizes; youngsters and adults. They spilled out of Greenacres Hill into the north side of town. Luza and I spotted four in St John's church graveyard, and Luza's mum moaned that there had been two inside the church during the Sunday service.

One day in Tesco, I noticed five dark grey ones in the vegetable aisle. A supermarket worker shooed them out using a broom. Three days later, a friend showed me a photo of a dozen in the entry lobby of the local cinema.

I told Luza: 'Your dream has come true.'

'I'm not sure that's a good sign,' she said.

I fretted, too. Where was this all headed?

Attitudes to the rabbits hardened in town. Before, people had mostly been pleased to see them. Now, they complained; demanded the council *do something*; even swore at the animals or pushed them off the pavement. Some elderly folk stopped going out for fear of tripping over them. Luza, although still on the rabbits' side, had to admit that using her mobility scooter was getting more difficult.

Apart from an occasional yowl if threatened, the rabbits were gentle. If I shooed them out of the way, they obliged meekly. Their sheer volume troubled me, though. I lived in a third-floor studio flat near Greenacres Hill and had a view over the town. As the weeks went on, I could see the sprawl of rabbits spreading like a furry cancer. I would stare, wondering: *how many more?* Luckily, the rabbits never made it up to my flat, but they did trouble the ground floor flats and houses.

Luza's mum, Mags, rang me at 7.45 am one day to say she'd woken to a living room full of them. 'Could you come round and help, Sophie?'

Because Luza got ill five years ago, at age twenty-three, she still lived with her mum, a few roads down, in a semi-detached cottage. I knew the place well, as I'd stayed many a night here as a teenager.

'Christ,' I said. Rabbits had invaded the living room. Luza was lying on the sofa, where she spent much of the day, petting several of them. There were more on the armchairs and side table, and it smelled all earthy. 'How did they get in?'

Mags shot a look at Luza. '*Someone* left a window open last night in the kitchen "by mistake".' The air quote marks suggested Luza was fibbing. 'How do I get rid of them?'

'Let's keep them, Mum,' said Luza. 'Go on.'

'I'm not having them in the house. What shall we do?'

I picked one up – it didn't struggle – and carried it out of the front door, giving it a stroke before putting it down. It sat there obediently. Five minutes later, Mags and I had taken them all outside.

'Shoo.' Mags waved her hands.

The rabbits hopped off down the road.

'Well, that was easier than I thought,' she said. 'Like a cuppa, love?'

'I have to get to work,' I told her.

***

Soon, there were over a thousand rabbits. The council removed them in van loads, but as quickly as they did so, more appeared. Occasionally, morning broke on Greenacres Hill and a few were bludgeoned to death.

'Jesus. How could anyone do that to bunnies?' said Luza.

Some people in town insisted that we get used to the rabbits. They shrugged and said, 'It's just how things are now.'

Once I might have sided with them; now I agreed with Luza.

'I've got a bad feeling about this.' She pressed a hand to her gut. 'What if they are *literally* the rabbits of the apocalypse?'

I didn't scoff this time. I shivered. 'More needs to be done.'

'Let's write to our MP for a start.'

The MP didn't live in town. His vaguely worded reply said he was, 'Keeping abreast of the issue' and 'All options were under consideration'. What rubbish!

In the library, I researched 'giant rabbit infestations in England', with no luck. I attended a meeting of the newly formed Anti-Rabbit League and wasn't keen – they were hot-tempered and all talk, no action. I helped a group trying to create rabbit-free zones. I spent my days off bundling several animals at a time into my car and then dumping them out in the countryside.

Nothing had any effect.

Mrs Spiller, from the ground floor of my block, came up to tell me she was off to stay with her brother down south, 'Until the rabbit problem is dealt with'. Mr and Mrs Patel, from the first floor, put their flat on the market, intending to move to a neighbouring town, but property prices had plummeted and the estate agent cautioned them that little was selling.

By now, it was common to wade through half an aisle of rabbits in Tesco. At the clinic where I worked, we often had to carry out animals that snuck in when no one was looking.

I thought about Luza's dream of drowning in an ocean of them.

***

The day I woke to find four large black ones on my sofa, like a fluffy portent, an icy fear swept through me. I had left no windows open. How the hell had they got in? From my window, I could see millions of them. In places, they looked two or three deep, clambering over each other. The animals possessed an unstoppable fleecy momentum. As I stared out, my limbs trembled.

I phoned Luza to check on her. Her voice was stifled – as if her throat was strained – when she told me her latest dream.

'They multiply into a rabbit city, then a bunny continent, then a furry planet in which all other life forms, including ours, suffocate.'

Bubble

In the park, the largest bubble she'd ever seen rose up and up. A massive orb glinting with hints of rainbow colours. She couldn't work out where it had come from, but this didn't surprise her. She had little idea of many things these days. A few years back, so much had seemed clearer, more comprehensible. Now the world fell on her in an odd way. And today she was here in the park, watching an enormous bubble drift into the sky.

'Bubble,' said a voice. The woman turned to see a man with white hair and a Bearded Collie on a lead. 'Bubble,' he said again, as if making sure the word sounded real.

'Yes.' She offered him a gentle smile.

'I don't know,' he said. 'I mean, you don't always know...'

'You don't.'

They both stared up at the bubble. It was high now, moving across the face of a cloud.

'Only came to the park on a whim today. Normally, I walk the dog by the river. Now I've seen the bubble,' he said.

'You have.'

'Sounds silly, but I don't want it to vanish from view. Ever.'

'It will.'

'I know. I don't want it to.'

'No.'

They stretched their heads back, gazing. The bubble got smaller and smaller, shrinking to a dot in the sky.

'Imagine. Something so big, improbable, marvellous, becomes... a point in the distance,' he said.

'That's perspective,' she said.

'That's everything,' he said.

Gardening with the Messiah

Agnes Carrington found the Messiah at the bottom of her garden, near a bed of flowering annuals. She recognised him from pictures she'd seen in the paper. He was sitting cross-legged, dressed in jeans and a Marvin Gaye tee-shirt, and smoking a roll-up cigarette. Curtains of greying hair and a bushy beard framed his face.

'Goodness,' she said, putting down her watering can. 'Hello.'

'Hi.' His smile was like a soft wash of late-afternoon sun.

'I've heard about you.'

'Oh?' Leaves from the ash tree, swaying in the summer breeze, cast flickering shadows across his face.

'You're that Messiah, aren't you?'

'I guess so.' He took a drag on his cigarette and then exhaled the smoke.

Her stomach fluttered. 'So what are you doing here, if you don't mind me asking?'

'Oh, this and that.'

She cleared her throat. 'I meant here in my garden.'

'I'd been told it was pretty.' He gestured around with a hand and smiled. 'It *really* is.'

'Well, I came to sort out this flower bed.' Agnes pointed it out. 'Would a Messiah help with that?'

'Of course.'

'Thank you.'

He leaned forward and stubbed out his cigarette on some soil, then tidied the butt away into a tin he kept in his jeans pocket and stood up. The man was tall and thin, with a slight paunch.

Agnes knelt, adjusting her position so that her bad right hip didn't hurt. With her gardening gloves on, she plucked weeds from one side of the bed. The

Messiah, who had wide hands with stubby fingers, worked on the other side and seemed wholly focused on the task. Agnes remembered gardening in this way with Marco, her husband. A tear came to her eye, but she willed her grief away, not wanting to trouble the Messiah.

'Aren't the coneflowers pretty?' she said.

'Yes. Some of your cosmos daisies need deadheading. Shall I do that?'

'Please.'

He set to work on the flowers.

Should she make small talk? That might not be a Messiah sort of thing. 'You preach, do you?' she asked.

'Some call it that.'

'Do any miracles?'

'So they say.'

For thirty minutes, they worked on the bed diligently and quietly. Agnes was always happiest when gardening, since caring for her plants gave her the impression that she was accomplishing something useful in her day. With the Messiah near, she felt a strange sense of calm, too.

Her hip ached, so she stood up. 'Can I offer you tea and cake?'

'Yes, please.'

Agnes showed the Messiah into the conservatory. 'The bathroom is through there if you want to clean up.' She pointed it out. 'And afterwards, please take a seat.'

She scrubbed her own soiled hands in the kitchen sink, and then she made tea in her blue china pot, unused since Marco's death eighteen months earlier. She brought out a chocolate cake. 'Is this okay?'

'Mm. Looks nice.'

They sat quietly, drinking and eating. Outside, a blackbird sang an aria, while foxgloves nodded sagely. The Messiah's tranquil presence reminded Agnes of an old church. She loved the companionable silence because she had had little of it since Marco died, and she didn't care for gossip, anyway. Her gaze was tugged to the silver cross that her husband, a practising Catholic, had hung on the wall. How she missed him!

The Messiah twice dropped crumbs down his beard and didn't notice. Agnes wondered whether to mention it, but decided on tact.

Eventually, Agnes said, 'Are you finished?'

'Yes, thanks. That was excellent.' He stood. 'I should be off now.'

'I'll show you to the door.'

'If you don't mind, I'll go out through the garden. That's more private.'

'But the gate's locked, and the fence is tall.' Agnes frowned. How had he even got into her garden? How daft that it had only just occurred to her to wonder that.

'Don't worry. There are a few advantages to being who I am.'

'Only a few?'

'Yes, a few.'

Outside, the sunshine haloed his head. 'This is a beautiful garden. So very English. You and your late husband created something wonderful here,' he said.

How on earth did he know Marco was dead? She'd said nothing. A miracle! 'Thank you.'

The Messiah's feet didn't quite touch the ground as he walked down the lawn. Or did they? She blinked because she was unsure. When he slipped behind the bushes at the base of the garden, Agnes lost sight of him.

How wonderful to have met the Messiah!

Agnes told her son, who visited later, that the Messiah had helped her do the garden.

'Your imagination is getting overactive again, Mum,' he said. 'It isn't healthy to be here on your own so much.'

She shook her head at his obtuseness and planted the memory in a flower bed of her mind.

Disillusioned by Mermaids

The sun presses warm to the barnacle of my morning. I stare out to sea, longing for glimpses of tails or heads breaching the surface, but see only choppy water.

Young Joe McFennan trudges towards me on the beach, with that battered plastic lobster he clutches sometimes. A short lad with a sweet face, he meets my gaze when he gets close. 'The mermaids,' he says. 'Have you seen them cavort yet in the crucible of the ocean?'

'Not this year,' I say.

'But they always come in May.' Hands on hips, he gazes out to sea.

'I really hope it's soon.'

He examines my face. 'You look like you need to dig.' He points to a wooden sign planted in the sand nearby, and then bids me goodbye and ambles off.

The sign says: *Please Dig Here*. I crouch down slowly, ensuring I don't aggravate the arthritis in my back. With cupped fingers, I scoop out handfuls of sand, making a hole. Is there a plaque buried here inscribed with Tara's arcane murmurs from when we first met? I dig and dig, like I'm searching for seahorses in a silent box.

I stop, puffing out a breath. Only sand.

I brush the tiny grains off my hands and glance up. Just below the cliff top are caves accessible via a steep staircase; people high on the Yellow Pages have written graffiti in them. Sometimes I visit the caves, but I don't fancy that staircase today. And the graffiti says nothing I don't already know – commercial sonnets, administrator haikus, and telephone numbers of relationship counsellors.

I continue along the beach, which reminds me of Tara when we first got together seven years ago, when I'd recently moved up from the south. We took long walks here, talking about the overtures of whales, laughing about how seals curtsey to clouds. Now domesticity has settled over us like a cloud of vaporised bread crumbs, so she takes Moonie for an early morning walk in the woods, then is busy writing in her office until late afternoon. I come here alone if I want a constitutional.

I head to the top of the beach where there are sheds, boats, fishing nets, and old buoys. The tourist shack sells gifts for the mermaids and paraphernalia about them – books on their myths and legends, hand-held mirrors, chocolates and marshmallows in watertight bags, hair extensions, and photographs of the mermaids on the rocks. A sign says: *Boat Trips to Spot the Mermaids with Storyteller Jo Mersea, 2 pm on Saturdays and Sundays. Sightings/Singing Not Guaranteed.*

I've heard Jo on local radio talking about the mermaids and playing recordings of them singing. She claims there have been sightings of them on this coastline for over 250 years.

Tara dismisses my interest in them, though. 'You're such a fantasist. Why do you still bother with mermaids at our age?' she says.

Does she have a point? Maybe. That mermaids exist makes the world more magical, doesn't it? Plus, unlike her, I've never seen one up close. I walk down towards the shoreline, the crisp wind a confessional on my face. Up above, gulls wheel in circles, and cirrus clouds drape across the cerulean sky.

The beach is half sand, half pebble. Meg Brewis, an acquaintance of Tara, is lying on a tartan blanket on the sand, her eyes shut against the warm sun. She opens her lids as I go past.

'Hi Meg,' I say. 'Are you dreaming of the mermaids?'

'No, of long corridors where fireflies flit.'

'Oh?'

'The mermaids.' She makes a dismissive sound, *tch.*

I look away and continue on.

At the end of the beach, I take the narrow path that leads around the rocky headland. Clusters of pink sea thrift dot the track, and the ocean stretches out pewter and glittering in the distance. After about ten minutes, as I turn a corner, I stop abruptly. Two mermaids are on the rocks about five metres away. Their scaly, muscular tails, about four feet in length, are stretched in front of them like premonitions of blue-green. My heart flips a Catherine wheel. It is very rare to see them this close up on land. They usually avoid the places where people visit.

Both mermaids have sunburnt skin. The older, plump one has long, lank, greying hair. The younger, thinner one with matted auburn hair has her arms folded and a tail that slaps at the rock irritably. I refrain from looking at their naked, sagging breasts. 'Greetings to you, mermaids, and to the breath of your indelible song,' I say.

They shoot each other a glance. The younger mermaid's mouth tightens. 'Why do you lot talk so weirdly?' Her accent is northern.

I'm unsure how to respond. What do you say to mermaids, anyway? 'I'm afraid I've brought no mermaid snacks for you.'

'I need antibiotics, not snacks.' The older one scratches at her tail, grimacing. 'A cut is infected.'

'I'm sorry.' My palms sweat. Seeing the mermaids has set my inner hummingbird tingling. 'Will you be singing soon, pledging illumination to the sky?'

The younger one picks at a scab on her arm. 'Doubt it.'

'Our singing is overrated,' says the other.

'But I've heard recordings. Your singing is a tuning fork of stars.'

The young one rolls her eyes. 'My singing is rubbish.'

'It really is.' Pressing her hands over her ears, the older mermaid makes a pained face. 'Fish, seals, crabs – all dash for cover when she sings.'

I chuckle – she is funny.

Tara, who has lived up here for over fifty years, has told me that mermaids are drip-dried in the mundane. Why was I reluctant to believe her? I hover, unsure whether to speak again.

'You humans don't half gawp.' The younger one's face is sour.

'You'd like me to go?' I ask.

'Yes,' says the older one.

'We're not museum exhibits,' says the younger.

91

I'm disappointed but try to let the feeling go. After all, I wouldn't appreciate people staring at me. I turn around and return along the same pathway. Sediment settles on my mental outcrop as the crag of my fantasy erodes. Tara is right. Mermaids aren't the mystical beings I want them to be. They simply are what they are, jaded by the sounds of it.

As soon as I get a phone signal back on the beach, I text Tara: *Just seen two mermaids close up.*

Whoopee, comes the sarcastic reply. *Did they sing to you?*

No.

Are you disillusioned ;)?

Yes. One made me laugh, though.

Isn't that as good as it gets, disillusionment but with some humour?

A pointed statement; she's got a point.

Fancy lunch at The Whalebone? I've finished my latest chapter, she texts.

The doorway of my step opens up. She is in a happy mood for once, so it'll be fun. We'll eat, drink wine, and chat like we can sometimes.

Sounds great, I text.

I head back to my car, the humdrum illumination of the familiar beckoning.

Duskers

In the mirror, my skin seemed an odd colour. A greyish hue with a pearly tint? Faintly transparent? How absurd that sounded. The word 'Dusker' flew to mind, but I shoved that thought away. I knew about Duskers – I'd occasionally notice one in the street, a spectral human form against a doorway, and feel unsettled. But become one myself? No way. I was too driven.

Even though it was midday on a Sunday, I'd only just dragged my sorry self out of bed. I was exhausted and achy with a tight chest. I'd had a nasty virus and while the fever had passed, I was still unwell.

The following day, the GP gave me the results of my basic blood tests. 'Everything's fine,' he said. 'Maybe you're simply stressed now, Helena.'

'Stressed?' I said in disbelief. 'I'm a fitness freak – I usually go to the gym every day – but even lifting dumbbells for ten minutes at home leaves me tired.'

'Your tests show nothing's wrong.'

'You know my boyfriend, Wenson, works as a physio here?' Said to get him to listen.

'Yes. Which is why I'm being frank.'

I left feeling annoyed with him.

After another week, Wenson said, 'Why not push yourself a little? You've probably lost fitness.'

Perhaps he had a point as a physiotherapist. So I attempted a gentle jog on Saturday. I only got halfway down the road before my leg muscles seized and breathlessness overtook me. I pushed on but was soon forced to stop, too weak, my chest pounding like I'd sprinted 200m. My smartwatch told me my heart rate was 158. *Christ.* I slumped on the ground until it settled. I was used to taking my body for granted; it was a vessel and a vehicle, not a broken-down heap that could betray me.

I spent the rest of the weekend in bed, with a strange pressure in my chest. Wenson brought me blueberry smoothies. His pale blue Nike t-shirt was the colour of his eyes, and his black tracksuit pants matched his eyelashes. With a finger, he stroked the tattoo on my biceps – a love heart pierced by a dumbbell. We'd lived in this tiny rented flat in the city for eighteen months, after matching on a dating app the year before. We both loved sessions at CrossFit gym and watching trashy horror films.

I was no shirker, so I kept going to work, even though I was unnaturally tired. By late morning, I'd have to read an email three times to retain it. During lunch breaks, I bunked off to a local church to lie on a pew and rest. Once, I heard a voice exclaim, 'Oh.'

My eyes jerked open, and I sat up. A Dusker was standing at the pew end. A tall black woman in a loose-fitting lilac dress, who was see-through as if reduced to about 35% opacity in Photoshop. Her thick dark eyeliner flicks made her seem young, but her transparency made it hard to judge her age. I had never spoken to a Dusker, so found myself stupidly tongue-tied.

'This is my usual pew,' she said.

Did she mean in which to pray? 'Oh?'

'You look like crap, by the way.'

'Cheers.'

'I wasn't being offensive. You aren't well, are you?'

How odd to be seen by someone who wasn't entirely visible herself. Weeks of pent-up emotion burst, and I ended up spewing a bit of my story.

'Take time off work,' she advised.

'The doctor claims there's nothing wrong.' It was strange talking to a woman who you could see through, right to the pew behind.

'Pah! They always say crap like that. They know zero about us.'

'Us?'

'People who get illnesses they don't understand.'

94

Overwhelmed by the urge to leave, I thanked her and legged it. Only later did I realise I hadn't asked her name.

Why hadn't I paid Duskers much heed before? Probably because they weren't easy to see, and I'd assumed they brought their condition on themselves. I knew Duskers existed in past eras – they were mentioned in my school history books – but being like that in modern times surely indicated a weak or negative character.

I took a week off as a 'holiday'. I holed up in bed, feeling a little perkier if I did nothing; resting recharged my batteries. I'd get up and stare in the mirror. I still thought my skin had a whisper of transparency, and remembering the Dusker, I shivered. When Wenson came home each night, I'd admit I hadn't been up to cooking. I was usually our chef.

'I'll make us something,' he'd say.

I returned to work despite worsening health, but after four weeks I was so knackered and weak, akin to a smartphone with only 10% battery life left. Even walking down the road was like wading through water, and pain stabbed at my quadriceps. A more sympathetic GP, Dr Wallenberg, signed me off with a sick note and did a few more tests, which turned up no obvious abnormalities. Then she handed me the business card of Netty Breakneck, a naturopath. 'Why not try her?'

Netty Breakneck's immaculate makeup complimented her brusque manner. After taking a case history, she told me there was nothing to worry about. 'You have a post-viral illness, but you're slim and basically fit, so you'll be right as rain in a few months.'

Relief flooded over me. I ignored the exorbitant cost of the consultation, although secretly I named her Netty Breakbank. A sackful of supplements accompanied me home. I did everything she suggested, including avoiding certain foods, and had confidence in what she called my 'journey to healing'. By the second month of treatment, I could go for a walk a few times a week, which made me feel foolishly invincible.

I pushed myself to resume work. During my first three weeks back, my chest got steadily tighter and my muscles throbbed and grew more numb with fatigue. My mind totally scrambled as I composed an email one day, the last time I went in.

On bad days now, I was pinned to the bed with weakness. Even thinking was shattering. My arms and thighs were thick with pain; my chest felt weighted down, as if an invisible Labrador was sprawled on me. Fog lodged in my brain, hoovering words from my memory, making me forget where I had put things down.

Netty visited me at home, telling me I was having 'a healing crisis' and to believe in recovery.

'Is getting better contingent on belief?' I croaked.

'Don't become a Dusker.'

'What?'

'Duskers are people whose vital presence becomes depleted by blocks in their energy fields.'

Despite her talking nonsense, I said, 'I won't become a Dusker.'

After she went, I Googled Duskers on my phone. I couldn't find much reliable information, but I came across the social media accounts of Duskers with lots of followers. Duskstar Debs made Tiktoks in her bedroom. 'It's more common than you imagine to turn translucent after a misfortune – a nasty infection, even a car accident,' she said. 'There are many people like me with a disabling physical condition for which no adequate tests or treatments exist.' Ellie B ranted in Instagram videos about Duskers' lack of media coverage and poor treatment by society: 'Just because we're transparent doesn't mean we shouldn't be seen or treated fairly… Many of us can't work or face discrimination from employers.' Her posts got umpteen likes, as well as comments that she was a 'benefits scrounger'. One disturbing video showed her being refused a table at a restaurant with a *No Duskers* sign on the door.

I closed my phone and put it out of my mind.

The next few months brought new symptoms: headaches, insomnia, mouth sores, night sweats, and swollen glands. I ached all over. Wenson often arrived home late from work, stinking of beer. When we spent time together on weekends, he quickly got to the point of fidgeting with his hoodie zip while an ugly pinch formed between his brows. I was in a parallel world to many friends, too, a wasteland to their playground, and I found it hard to go on Instagram. My friends received innumerable likes for posting daily gym selfies while I would largely be ignored with an occasional post about my nuked health.

Out of the blue, Wenson announced he was off on holiday with his best friend. 'A break will do us good.'

'It'll do *you* good, you mean?'

'Don't start. It's booked now.'

I refused to show him I was upset when he left, and alone in the flat, I relaxed. The guilt that I wasn't pulling my weight eased. I missed him, though.

Mum, who lived up north, took two weeks off her job and came down to help. At first, she kept asking if everything was okay with Wenson. Then, seeing me shake after the exertion of taking a bath or struggling to walk up the stairs, she realised something was seriously wrong. 'Aren't there more tests the doctor can do?'

'She says not.'

'We need to get to the bottom of this. It's like... you're vanishing a little.'

I glanced in the mirror and understood that Mum was right. Previously, my clothes had appeared normal when on, but now they took on the subtle translucency of my skin. A spectre looked back at me, even if I wasn't see-through. A lump came into my throat.

Mum hugged me. 'I'm here, my love.'

My eyes blurred with tears. How overwhelming! Severe sickness had shoved my life into a strange shredder yet my boyfriend and many friends didn't seem to care. At least I had Mum.

She offered to pay for me to see a private immunologist, so I booked an appointment. I began more online research, finding support groups on social media. Rest, pace myself, try various supplements and learn meditation techniques – my best bets, apparently. I stopped seeing Netty Breakbank.

When Wenson returned from the holiday, looking hot, he told me he was leaving me. I hadn't seen that coming. I dropped to the ground and burst into tears.

'Please don't.' He wouldn't look at me. 'I can still help now and then with practical stuff until you're completely better.'

'How gracious of you,' I said sarcastically.

He packed some of his things and told me he'd return for the rest. He eyed the door. 'Try to push yourself more, Helena. It'll help you.'

My eyes widened in shock. 'Don't you think I'd do that if it was humanly possible?'

He left without another word. I smashed his favourite mug, the one that said *I'd Rather Be at the Gym*.

The tears fogged my vision for months. But it wasn't only the breakup. It was the way I'd been sucked into an existential washing machine, churned around, and then vomited out into a grimy cellar of reality. I'd always handled stressful times by running. How to cope when I was too shattered and in pain to exercise at all? And why was there no medical understanding when my body was this horrendously sick?

One hot July day, I dragged myself to the bench about thirty metres down on my street. Without a garden, I needed some fresh air. I lay flat on the bench, no longer caring what the neighbours thought.

'We meet again,' said a voice.

I sat up and noticed the Dusker I'd seen in the church, wearing a lime-green summer dress. Due to their transparency, Duskers resembled their surroundings and being partially a Viburnum hedge heightened her beauty.

'Are you resting?' she said.

'Yup.'

'I'll rest bleeding anywhere these days, too.' She cackled a rebellious sound.

I smiled. 'I'm Helena. You?'

'Leona. Shove up.'

She sat next to me. I shared a little of my story. She told me she had developed her illness, and later her transparency, five years back, after a series of nasty infections.

'You've been ill that long?'

She nodded. 'But don't worry. Many post-viral problems resolve on their own within a year or so. Only the unlucky sods like me develop a more serious disease.'

'There's nothing anyone can do?'

She let out a breath. 'You grow up thinking doctors are there to help. With chronic illness, that's not always the case. They can be dismissive and gaslighting.'

That resonated with my experience of Wenson, which still stung. 'So is becoming a Dusker irreversible?'

'For many, yes, but some do recover their opaqueness over time. There's no rhyme or reason to it.'

Leona seemed like a strong person. I wondered if I'd misjudged Duskers. 'Are you a typical Dusker?'

'What's that supposed to mean?'

'Sorry.'

'Look. We're just people who have mystery illnesses, ones tricky for medics and families to acknowledge. Not culturally legitimate diseases where you get proper support and treatment. Healthy folk are freaked out by us because they can't handle the fact that *anyone* ultimately can become a Dusker.'

Might it happen to me? Though I was a little more gauzy than two months ago, I wasn't a full-blown, see-through Dusker.

'Perhaps you should go home. You look rough,' she said.

99

When I first became sick, the cherry tree outside my flat had been in bloom. Now its leaves lay on the ground. Who was I these days? I felt like a stranger in an unknown city, one without landmarks or road names.

Many friends had stopped contacting me and I was becoming more unnoticed in the world, too. My shopping was mostly delivered, but if I occasionally made it to the corner shop, I'd have to clear my throat to be seen and served.

I didn't have that problem with the private immunologist, though, an attentive man who resembled a thin Idris Elba. He gave me antiviral drugs and some supplements to try, but unless I paid £2000 for specialist blood tests, he couldn't recommend further treatments (which offered no guarantees, anyway). That was way over my budget. So his advice was to pace myself, not push myself, and he told me that some patients improved slowly over time.

Work was getting bolshy, so I applied for sickness benefits. Before, I'd assumed they were easy to claim. The reality was a gruelling eye-opener – the huge form to fill in and then the long interview where I felt on trial for a crime. Luckily, I was granted it.

The extreme exhaustion and crushing muscle pain swaddled me in gloom, slipped blinkers on me, so everything seemed filtered through it. On slightly better days, when it was less bone-shattering, I lay in bed sketching female figures in crosshatched interiors on a pad. The act of drawing lifted me.

One day, slouched on the bench along my street, I heard, 'We must stop meeting like this.'

My heart rose upon seeing Leona. In the autumn light, her translucent figure had a copper glow – or was that the colour from the dying hedge behind? She looked stunning.

'Shove up.' She sat by me. 'How are you?'

'You know.' I shrugged.

'Yes, I do.'

We chatted, and then I said, 'Can I ask you something personal?'

'Fire away.'

'How does being transparent feel?'

She pondered. 'Not sure I have the words, but my body, once familiar, feels alien now that it's sick. It's… uncanny. Or like I'm part of my body but not part of it, all at once. Does that make any sense?'

I thought of the disease as an alien presence in my body. 'I guess so.'

'I feel invisible to most people, like I don't exist anymore – or like they can't see how disabled and sick I am.'

'Tell me about it.'

'You're faintly transparent yourself. Does that feel like anything?'

I considered it. 'Sometimes it doesn't feel like anything much, except that I ache all over. Sometimes I'm more absent than present in myself.'

'Has your poo become see-through?' Leona chuckled. 'At first, mine wasn't, then it was.'

'No.' I laughed, too. 'Is yours?'

'Yes.' She cackled some more.

We chatted, and I asked where she lived.

'Number 18B, towards the other end of the street, if you ever want to visit. Let me give you my text number.'

Six weeks later, I made it to her front door. She walked before me up to her first-floor flat, a ghostly shape against the staircase. Even spectral, she looked funky in her turquoise dress.

The living room was crammed with books, a vinyl collection, glass bowls, indoor plants, trinket dishes, and other clutter. Art posters covered the walls. *Your Body is a Battleground* declared one.

'Lie there.' Leona indicated one of the two sofas. 'Fancy some green tea?'

'Please.'

She returned with mugs and then laid on the other sofa. I watched to see, when she sipped her tea, if the liquid was visible in her throat, but as soon as it left her mouth, it blended into her transparent body.

We shared stories, and I liked her sarcasm. 'Wenson Blue? That's not a name, it's a pornstar character,' she said.

I laughed.

She told me about other Duskers – a network of them who campaigned on social media. 'Did you hear Ellie B got arrested for sneaking into the empty Houses of Parliament? She did a live Instagram about the prejudice against Duskers, sitting on the government bench. That woman rocks!'

Leona and I began hanging out once every three months or four months, all we could manage health-wise. We would moan, laugh, discuss treatments and supplements we were trying, and share fears. She encouraged me to keep drawing.

'That's awesome,' she said, looking at my sketch of her.

***

The cherry tree had bloomed four times since I'd first got that flu. I was no better. I'd made innumerable attempts to get back into life, but the more I did, the more I hurt to my bones and deteriorated further. It took time to learn that lesson.

At 10 am, I was under my duvet. Light filtering through an indigo glass vase painted a pretty spectrum of blue hues on the windowsill. My illness had stilled me and made me more of an observer, even if it was an unenviable life.

I got up and stared in the mirror. 'I'm a Dusker,' I said to my transparent reflection. I'd discovered that far from being weak, we Duskers were so strong just to hold it together and exist. Running a marathon was a doddle compared to being eternally sick and housebound. I'd become politicised too, posting about Dusker issues on social media. I'd learned about Duskers who were bedridden 24/7, unable even to sit up. The government spent next to no money on researching our condition, leaving us to rot.

I got a taxi to the local park for a very rare outing with Leona. There were advantages to blending in with the scenery. We played the 'Suss the Healthy Person' game, sidling up unnoticed close to a couple on a bench, laying on the grass behind them and listening to their conversation. From a distance, they'd appeared intimate, holding hands, but closer up gave me a different impression.

We moved away. 'I don't think he listens to her, and she's unhappy,' I said.

'I agree. She should tell him to do one,' said Leona.

We thought of ourselves as akin to the angels in *Wings of Desire*. Being a Dusker seemed to attune us more to what was happening inside people. We liked to believe we could see through Healthies psychologically, as they could see through us physically. Perhaps that was why we made them uncomfortable. Or was it that we reminded them how precarious life is?

Then Leona and I played another game – sitting hidden in the shade of an oak tree, freaking out strangers by reciting song lyrics as they passed. We only ever pranked men, and this one resembled Wenson. The jogger jerked his head around, wondering where that voice had come from, then shrugged and continued. Leona and I caught each other's eye and laughed.

Gone with the Gypsies

When Alan entered the lounge, his white-haired mother stared up at him from her armchair. 'Who are you?' she said.

I should be used to this, but it still gets to me. 'I'm Alan, Mum. Your son. Remember?'

'Have you come about the heads?'

He sighed inwardly. 'The heads?'

She leaned forward, saying in a hushed tone, 'They're growing heads in the garden next door.'

'They're pumpkins. Told you that before, Mum.'

'Liar. They're heads,' she snapped.

'Okay. You're right. No need to worry about them.'

She tugged at her cardigan sleeve. 'You must tell next door to stop growing heads.'

'Told them already. They'll stop soon.'

'You must tell them, you must!'

He held up his hands, baring his palms. 'Okay. I'll go now.'

Outside the house, Alan exhaled a long breath. He glanced at his watch and saw that it was 3.30 pm. He'd let a few minutes pass before returning inside, though by that time she may have forgotten about the heads, anyway.

He'd already been through this pretence several times. On the first occasion, he'd gone next door, asking Julie if she'd erect a screen so his mother wouldn't see the pumpkins. Julie obliged, placing wooden boxes in front of them, but that upset his mother even more. 'They've put a coffin around the heads so they can't breathe now. The heads must sing when the flowers die.' Alan's mother sang out, 'The Lord is my-y shepherd...'

'Shush, Mum, I'll sort it out.'

104

He returned to Julie's house, asking her to remove the boxes. The pumpkin season would be over in a matter of weeks, anyway.

Today, an icy breeze prickled Alan's bald head. He patted his upper arms with his palms to keep warm. A tiny hole marred one sleeve of his royal blue jumper and, frowning, he picked at it. Had it been a mistake so soon after retiring to take on looking after his mother? It'd seemed sensible at the time. Eleanor and he had been separated for years, while Janie had her own family up in Edinburgh. But he awoke each day with dark ribbons in his thoughts and heaviness in his chest.

Alan trudged up the driveway to the bare oak on Magdalene Street. He poked a toe into the yellow leaves scattered beneath the tree, and the aroma of mildew tickled his nose. He used to find a tender nostalgia in the colours and fallen leaves of autumn, but the season felt shrunk to its core now – decay. Picking up an acorn, he turned it over in his long, slim fingers before chucking it down.

A chilly breeze made Alan shiver. He checked the time – 3.35 pm – and paced back inside with a leaden heart. 'I had a word with next door about the heads,' he said to his mother. 'They'll take them away soon.' He forced a smile, hoping she might grin back.

Her brow crinkled. 'Are you the person who gives me my tea?'

A spurt of irritation. 'I'm Alan, your son.'

'Are you, dear?'

His mother's body, hunched in the high armchair, looked fragile. He remembered her sitting upright, eyes twinkling, as she told him that Leonard Cohen was a better songwriter than Bob Dylan – 'Dylan may have been the voice of his generation, but Cohen's a more intimate poet, closer to the heartstrings'; Alan had disagreed. He scarcely knew what to say to her these days and was relieved tea time had arrived. Tea was one of the few things left to share.

'Like some tea, Mum?'

'Tea? Yes, please.'

In the kitchen, he made two cups of tea using the royal blue china set he'd bought for his mother's eighty-fifth birthday. Back in the lounge, he placed one cup on her side table.

She stared at it. 'What's this? I don't think it belongs to me, dear.'

'Just tea,' Alan said firmly. 'Drink up.'

She nodded, frowned, nodded again, and smiled faintly, as if in silent conversation with herself. During times such as this, she didn't seem to notice his presence. Her slate-blue eyes were dull and opaque, like the flat grey pebbles on the nearby beach. The skin on her cheeks was so translucent that veins could be seen through it. *It's strange how the biological is being revealed while the psychological is retreating further and further away*. Alan shivered.

His mother turned her palms upwards and studied them, something she often did. 'You see, you have to follow the lines. Follow the lines and you understand... The lines show the buses and trains where to go. The buses and trains can get us there... You don't have scones and cream. No, no scones for you, Jones.'

Alan rubbed his temples with a palm. Who was Jones? This name came up in her ramblings. A childhood friend he'd never heard about, who became significant in her disintegrating mind? Although his mother had lost much of her short-term memory, her long-term memory was like a jigsaw puzzle with only certain pieces missing.

'No scones for you, Jones,' she repeated.

Alan popped into the kitchen to get the biscuit tin. He offered his mother the opened tin. 'Have a chocolate biscuit?'

'I can never resist chocolate.' She raised her brows as she smiled puckishly and then took one.

After five years, he'd resigned himself as much as he could to her dementia, but when the woman she once was resurfaced unexpectedly like this, sadness prodded at him, and he turned his face away in case she noticed it in his eyes.

106

The piano stood near the oak sideboard. He remembered her playing Nina Simone's 'My Baby Just Cares for Me' when he was a child. Her long, slender fingers would melt into the keys and her clean soprano voice would make warmth pool in his heart. After she finished, his mother would sit Alan on her lap, hugging him. 'You're my pumpkin pie,' she'd say.

Today, her fingers trembled as she held her teacup to her lips. Now was his time to make her feel safe. But how could you comfort someone who no longer knew what comfort meant?

***

Shafts of wan sunshine floated through the lounge window. An unfamiliar man paced through the door and Marianne frowned in confusion. 'Who are you?'

'I'm Alan, Mum, your son. Remember?'

Do I have a son? No, I don't think so. Maybe he was talking about the sun. Or was he here about the heads? 'Have you come about the heads?'

'The heads?'

'They're growing heads in the garden next door.' Marianne spoke quietly because the neighbour used a special device to listen in to her conversations.

'They're pumpkins. Told you that before, Mum.'

Surely he knew the heads could sneak into houses at night, with their eyes of flame and sharp triangular teeth. 'Liar. They're heads.'

'Okay. You're right. No need to worry about them.'

'You must tell next door to stop growing the heads.'

'Told them already. They'll stop soon.'

Why didn't he listen to her? Why would no one listen? 'You must tell them, you must!'

'Okay, I'll go right now.' The man exited the room.

She pressed a hand to her mouth, trying to remember. Who was he? Who?

Her attention shifted to the late afternoon sunshine, which dusted a bowl of oranges with coppery hues.

Oranges which come from far away … Jones came from far away in a curvy caravan ... and I loved him ... never told anyone ... never ... Mother said gypsies were common... Jones was unique, not common ... he knew the answer to rivers and the lines to follow ... the lines that take you there, that show you ... Gypsy Jones couldn't afford scones and cream ... and just when I meant to tell him ... but no more scones, not when he slipped away on moony roads.

A man appeared, disrupting her reverie. 'I've had a word with next door about the heads. They'll take them away soon.'

His slate-blue eyes were oddly familiar. 'Are you the person who gives me my tea?'

'I'm Alan, your son.'

'Are you, dear?' So she had a son. She remembered she hadn't tied the knot with Gypsy Jones, whom she'd adored. She'd married Mark, hadn't she?

'Like some tea, Mum?'

'Tea? Yes please.'

He left the room. She shifted in her chair, trying to get more comfortable. Her lower back and right thigh ached. She heard the long hiss of a kettle boiling.

He reappeared with a royal blue cup, which he put on the side table. She didn't like that shade of blue much. 'What's this? I don't think it belongs to me, dear.'

'Just tea,' he said firmly. 'Drink up.'

Her shoulders tensed. Why did people use that tone? Mark often spoke like that … *not Jones ... he was gentle, Gypsy Jones ... a soft voice speaking the things he loved ... the maps of buses and trains ... lines that take you there, where you can view statues of men or stars bathing in rivers ... at the end of that one ... and buses and trains ... or gypsy caravans travelling on moony roads ... Gypsy Jones never had scones and cream, too poor ... he read palms but much preferred the lines on maps.*

Marianne turned her hands over, looking at her palms. 'You see, you have to follow the lines. Follow the lines and you understand… The lines show the buses and trains where to go. The buses and trains can get us there… You don't have scones and cream. No, no scones and cream for you, Jones.'

She'd stolen scones and cream for Jones from her mother's kitchen; she'd teased him, 'No scones for you, Jones.'

A voice interrupted her thoughts. 'Have a chocolate biscuit?'

Her son held out the biscuit tin. 'I can never resist chocolate.' She grinned as she took one.

Yes, she recognised Alan now, even if he wasn't her child by Jones, who'd vanished with the gypsies just after she turned eighteen. He was Mark's son and a kind, thoughtful man.

Marianne had times like this when full awareness washed over her. It was then that fear gripped her, a vertiginous sensation, as if she were tumbling into space. *I'm losing my mind. I don't recognise my family, and I perceive things that aren't real.* She took a few deep breaths to try to calm herself. Then ate her chocolate biscuit for comfort.

At least Alan was here. Wasn't that the wrong way around? Shouldn't she, his mother, be supporting him? Selfishly, she wanted him around to make her safer.

Marianne followed his gaze to the piano. Leonard Cohen's raspy tenor came to her, singing lyrics she struggled to recall, something like, *I've forgotten so very much…*

As she picked up her teacup, her hand trembled. She reached her other hand under the cup for support. The lines on her palms were deep.

Yes, I forget so very much these days… even the lines… that take you there… that go… elsewhere? …

Acknowledgements

'Let Them Float' originally started as a 3000-word short story, 'Human Balloon', which came third in the Lucent Dreaming short story prize, 2021. It was later developed into a much longer story.

'The Rabbits of the Apocalypse', was first published in the MPT short story prize anthology, July 2022. Also shortlisted in the Exeter short story prize, 2022, and the To Hull and Back short story prize, 2023.

'Disillusioned by Mermaids' was first published in *Cafe Irreal*, #65, Winter 2018.

'Bubble' was first published in *The Casket of Fictional Delights,* May, 2016.

I want to thank Dot Schwartz, Petra McQueen, and Ruth Arnold for their feedback on various stories. Thanks also to Anne Hamilton and Verity Holloway for their excellent editing.

About the Author

Katy Wimhurst's first collection of short stories was *Snapshots of the Apocalypse* (2022, Fly on the Wall Press). Her fiction has been published in numerous magazines including *The Guardian, Cafe Irreal, Ouen Press,* and *ShooterLit.* She has won various short story competitions, including Tate Modern TH2058, *Writers' Forum* 2022, Crazy Cats 2023, and *EarlyWorks Press* 2018. Her visual poems have appeared in magazines like *Ric Journal, 3AM, Steel Incisors, Dreampop Press* and *The Babel Tower.* Her first book of visual poems, *Fifty-One Trillion Bits,* was published by Trickhouse Press (2023). She blogs at whimsylph.wordpress.com. She is housebound with the illness M.E.

Printed in Great Britain
by Amazon

28253622R00064